The Age o

CH

BY BRUC. ...RDS

Lambert Hill

Lambert Hill
P.O. Box 1478
Brea, CA 92822-1478
www.LambertHill.com

The Age of Amy: Channel '63

ISBN: 978-0-9837604-4-3 (print)
ISBN: 978-0-9837604-5-0 (ebook)

Song excerpts
Words and music by Bruce Edwards
Published by Lambert Hill (ASCAP)

Your Love, Like Music - © 2014
You Make Me Smile - © 1973
By The Time You Get This Letter - © 1973
As Long As You Come Back To Me - © 1973
What I'll Do For You - © 2014
The Jail Song - © 2014
Compassion - © 2014
Goodbye, Sweet Melody - © 2014
Bring Us Home, Sweet Mary - © 1972

Printed in the United States of America

www.AgeOfAmy.com

To

THE EDWARDS BROTHERS

The greatest '60s rock band you never heard of.

Contents

Chapter 1

Emancipation

"*I* quit!" I shouted, my shrill voice echoing through the courtroom. "I resign from this family!"

"Please take your seat, Amy," said Judge Higgins. "Your theatrics have been noted, but you are in Family Court, not an episode of *Law & Order.*"

The August sun blazed through the windows onto an empty jury box. There were no lawyers, no court reporters, nor spectators in the gallery. On this day, no testimony would be given from the witness stand. The judge didn't even have a gavel.

Judge Higgins shuffled a pile of legal documents on his tall desk, then set aside the papers that prompted this gathering in the first place: *Petition for Declaration of Emancipation of a Minor.* In our state the law permits minor children with parental issues to leave home and live with someone else. I was the minor in this case. I had petitioned the court to let me live on my own, to be liberated from playing the dutiful daughter, to be released from the grip of my pathetic parents. In simpler terms: I wanted a divorce from my family.

I had filed the papers all by myself, with no help from anyone. For sure, it was a bold move, especially for a 16-year-old.

My mom and dad sat at a long table normally reserved for high-powered attorneys. I sat at the same table, a few empty chairs down from them. After all, they were the bad guys, not me.

"As to why I called you all here," said the judge, "I want to see if we can resolve this issue before proceeding further with this case."

My dad raised his hand and rose to his feet. "What's the point?" he said. "We are all in agreement in this matter."

"Absolutely," added my mother. "Amy wants to move out, and I for one don't plan to stand in her way."

"I understand that," said Judge Higgins, "but before I can issue a ruling, the laws of this state and the Department of Social Services mandate that the court shall first attempt to mitigate the situation, in accordance with Family Code Regulations."

Legal mumbo jumbo! The "situation" was clear. I no longer wanted to share my life with my parents, and they made no bones about not wanting me around.

It was all perfectly legal. Separations between parent and child were graciously granted in cases involving abandonment, neglect, and maltreatment. Thoughtlessness and disrespect topped my list of grievances. As far as I was concerned it was an open-and-shut case. I wasn't even asking for financial support, although my folks could have easily afforded it.

None of this would have happened when I was younger. My first fifteen years had been pretty normal—even above average, I would say. My dad was a struggling writer, and Mom, a devoted mother and homemaker. Along with my elder brother and sister, we were the all-American, lower-middle-class family. We lived in a modest city apartment, and survived on Dad's meager earnings from whatever part-time work he could dig up.

With little to spend on entertainment, we made do with simple pleasures. Family outings rarely went beyond the city park around the corner. In winter I built slushy snowmen and crossed frozen ponds in secondhand skates. Summer ice cream cones were limited to single scoops. Watching the other kids devour fudge sundaes always left me feeling a little inferior, but a piggyback ride home on my dad's shoulders never failed to bring back a smile.

By all rights I should have felt cheated for having to suffer through a deprived childhood, but we were a close family then, and I loved every minute of it!

I gazed out the courtroom window while the judge rattled off more legal gibberish. He had to raise his voice at one point, over the rumbling of a tractor rolling past the cow pasture across the street.

That's right—a cow pasture! The city I loved was now a distant memory. Dad had found success in a string of best-selling novels he had authored. To escape his instant celebrity, he uprooted us to *Shankstonville*—a small farming community smack dab in the middle of America's heartland. It was a move I did not want to make, but what choice did I have?

Along with Dad's financial rewards came the trappings of wealth. All the things we had done without in years past were suddenly at our finger-tips. Dad bought a huge, opulent house behind tall, iron gates. An avalanche of material possessions rolled through our front door, and the more consumer goods flowed in, the more family values rushed out. My parents became possessed by their ultra-sized, big-screen TV. My brother and sister —and onetime playmates—stayed locked up in their rooms, lured into a cyber realm from where they would never return.

Everyone was content to hide from the world in that monstrous palace, but not me! I was the outgoing type, and craved involvement. I dyed a neon-blue streak in my hair as a form of protest. Lame, I know, but then I hadn't had much experience in rebellion.

I wanted out of that house, so I decided to take legal action to gain my independence. The only complication was where I was going to live next. My grandparents had passed away by then, and I had no other living relatives to take me in. But that didn't deter me. What I really wanted was to live by myself, but being under age, there was no way the judge was going to allow it. The only other option was that I be placed in foster care. Ugh!

"In light of there being no kin to take custody of Amy," said the judge, "and with no one else willing to assume guardianship, the court will have to rule based on what is best for the child."

"The best thing for her," said my dad, "is to give her what she wants. Let her face the world on her own terms, and learn how hard it *really* is. Struggling to earn an income would be a good lesson in humility. Let her feel the frustration of being short on rent each month."

"And what about having enough to eat?" said my mom. "Maybe experiencing hunger pains will make her appreciate what it takes to keep food on the table."

I stood up and faced the judge. "I never said living alone would be easy," I said. "But if you think that's not *'what's best for the child,'* think again! Place me in foster care, if that's what you're planning to do, but be prepared to have another runaway teen on your hands."

A faint buzzing sound came from the bench. A housefly was circling the judge's head. It zoomed in front of his face like a military drone on a bombing mission. The judge waved a legal pad at the fly, but it persisted in tormenting him. Finally, the fly buzzed over to a window and rested on the glass. Beyond it lay his freedom; to carouse with others of his own kind; to share a trash can lunch with his fellow pests. All someone needed to do was open the window and he would be free. I was looking for that same opening for myself, but like the fly, I was in a court of law, where justice isn't always guaranteed.

"I think I had better speak privately with the petitioner in my chambers," said Judge Higgins. "Come with me, Amy."

The only other time I could remember hearing the word "chamber" was in the *Chamber of Horrors* at a wax museum. I didn't really expect to see medieval torture devices on the walls of a dank dungeon, but I crept cautiously through the chamber door just the same. The room was a dark, windowless box, lined with bookshelves full of law books. It was musty and smelled like old shoes, probably because the courthouse was one of the oldest buildings in town.

The judge flipped on the ceiling light, then removed his black robe. Underneath he had on a Hawaiian shirt and shorts.

"Are we keeping you from something?" I asked him.

"It gets hot under that thing," he said, "especially in summertime, and I like to be comfortable while I'm working." He opened a small refrigerator in the corner. "Want some cold lemonade?"

"I would rather know what you wanted to see me about," I said.

"Mind if I have one?"

"Be my guest."

He cracked open his bottle and sat down at a desk in the middle of the room. Then he reached under the table and came up with an armful of legal folders.

"See these?" he said, plopping the papers onto the desktop. "Teenage runaways. Right now they're in a juvenile detention facility. They all thought they could make it as street kids. Every one of them has been assaulted and abused. When Juvenile Justice gets done with them, many will go to group homes. The lucky ones will be welcomed back with their families. Amy, once emancipation is granted, your folks are under no legal obligation to take you back. The state will regard you as an adult, and you'll be treated as such under the law. If things don't work out for you, you'll be on your own."

"I'll take my chances."

"That's what these kids thought, and they all became homeless. Do you have any idea what that's like? It means eating out of dumpsters, begging for handouts, being ridiculed, or worse!"

The judge's speech was starting to get to me, but I wasn't about to show it.

"What do you want me to do?" I asked.

"Reconsider," said the judge. "Talk to your parents. Work something out."

"Negotiate. Is that what you're asking me to do? Well, I'm not interested."

"Just because you're in court doesn't mean you can't call this whole thing off. It's a simple process to throw out your case, and I'd be happy to do it for you."

"Don't you get it? My family is screwed up!"

"A little dysfunctional, maybe, but that can be corrected."

"Look, Judge, I appreciate your concern, but if I wasn't absolutely sure about this, I wouldn't have filed the papers."

The judge sighed. "Alright, Amy. We'll move ahead with your case, but I'm going to require that you consult with an attorney." He jotted down an address and phone number on a note pad. *"Robert Phillips* specializes in Family Law."

"Who's gonna pay for *that?*"

"It will be done pro bono."

"Pro what?"

"That means it's free. Attorneys sometimes forgo fees to represent those who can't afford one. Bob was a well-respected family law attorney, and taught at several prestigious law schools before he retired. Helping families in crisis is his calling. I'll set you up an appointment with him."

Only the squeaky hinges of our front door made any sound. No one spoke a word as my parents and I crossed the threshold into our farmland mansion. The quiet wouldn't last long, however, as Mom and Dad planted themselves in front of their giant-screen TV. It was time for the afternoon block of talk shows. Then came their favorite reality program, *The Itch Factor*, where contestants are dusted with itching powder, then dropped in the middle of Time Square, butt-naked. Anyone caught scratching gets the boot.

As the TV volume ratcheted up, I climbed the mahogany staircase to my room. Down the hallway I heard the doors to my brother and sister's bedrooms slam shut. They had shown no interest one way or the other in my legal pursuits, preferring to hunker down in their rooms with their hi-tech devices, where what little brains they had left would be sucked out of them.

Passing my sister's room, I heard the distinct

sound of gossip over her smartphone. When she wasn't spreading ugly rumors with her vocal chords, she was typing them out on social media sites.

The sound of machine gun fire and bomb blasts leaked out under my brother's door. The consummate gamer, he spent all of his free time splattering virtual blood across his video screen.

At the end of the hallway, and a few more steps up, was my bedroom. It had once been the attic, but was converted into livable space to allow me the greatest distance from that annoying downstairs TV. Unlike the rest of my family, I was a voracious reader. Some people can read while listening to music through earbuds. I needed absolute silence.

I stepped over a welcome mat that I had rescued from our former city residence. It read *Enter at your own risk!* Back then it was meant as a joke. Our home was always open to visitors. Now it had quite a different meaning: Stay out!

I plopped down on my bed and turned on my bedroom TV. My day in court had left my mind in a fog, and I needed a diversion. I switched around the channels, past abusive judges, gushing talk show guests, and rude psychotherapists. Then I happened upon a channel that played nothing but reruns of old TV programs.

The *Andy Griffith Show* was on.

Having long been fascinated with the culture of

the 1960s, I never tired of the antics of Andy, Opie, and Barney. The episode was one I had seen many times before. Little Opie learns the meaning of death and renewal, when he releases the orphaned sparrows he had raised, into the wild. The emotional ending always chokes me up.

Then an episode of *Leave It to Beaver* came on.

As usual, the Cleaver household was spotless. The beds were made and the furniture was dusted.

"Hi, Mom! Hi, Dad!" said the slow-witted Beaver as he bounded down the stairs. His brother, Wally, followed behind him in his school varsity sweater. Dad relaxed on the couch with the morning paper, while Mom made lunch box sandwiches, in a dress and pearl necklace. It was amazing! I wasn't just watching a black and white show from a time well before my birth, I was eavesdropping on the simple, unhurried era of the early '60s.

Was life really like that back then? Possibly. It was a time of cheap housing, 20-cent-per-gallon gasoline, and full employment with a guaranteed pension. Families enjoyed home-cooked meals, courtesy of wives and mothers who rarely left the kitchen.

The show ended with the proverbial dinner table scene. There were the Cleavers, sitting with perfect posture, their feast tenderly prepared by Beaver's mom.

I muted the volume to escape the dreadful

dialog. Beaver might have been bragging about his earnings from mowing lawns that day. Wally could have been sharing his latest misadventures with bigmouth Eddie Haskell.

Then I noticed something I wasn't expecting. It was a trite scene, for sure. All the family shows back then had them. But while the Cleavers ate and conversed . . . they smiled! They looked at each other. I moved closer to the screen, finally realizing why the scene had so captured my imagination. These weren't just fictional characters providing comic relief to millions of Americans.

They were a *family*.

Chapter 2

Animal Attractions

*T*he dawn of a new day brought more questions than answers:

What if I am forced to live with foster parents?

What if I hate them?

What if I end up on the streets?

What if I die and nobody cares?

What if I run away with the circus?

What if I get trampled by elephants?

C'mon Amy, I said to myself, now you're getting stupid! You've always been good at figuring things out. Why are you having such a problem now?

I needed a place to think. More importantly, I needed to talk to someone my own age, who understood how I felt. The school year hadn't started yet, and I still had plenty of free time on my hands. So, I decided to spend the morning with my good friend Hubert, and take a break from my troubles for a while.

Like me, Hubert was once a city-dweller. We shared most of the same classes at school, the same love for reading, and listened to the same style of music (Jazz and Blues). The main difference between us was that he was smarter than me—an A-student, in fact. It was rare not to find his nose buried in a textbook, devouring its pages through his thick, pop bottle glasses. I, on the other hand, was into political activism and fighting for social change—things Hubert didn't feel deserved his attention. We were like two passengers on a ship at sea. I was at the helm steering the ship, while he was in the engine room seeing how it worked.

It was our differences that ruled out any chance of us ever becoming romantically involved. But Hubert was the kindest and most considerate boy I ever met—and the only person I knew with a drivers license.

When it comes to escaping reality, there's no better place to go than to *Theme Farm,* a theme park just outside of Shankstonville. Hubert and I both had annual passes that got us into the park, anytime we wanted. It was our favorite hangout.

"Sit well back in your seats, and keep your hands and arms inside at all times," said the loudspeaker voice on the parking lot tram. It was only a short ride to Theme Farm's main entrance, but long enough for Hubert to consume half-a-chapter of a book on *Molecular Orbital Theory.* He was reading from his

tablet computer, that you rarely saw him without.

Unlike my peers, I shunned those electronic gadgets that enslaved my generation.

"Put that thing down!" I told Hubert. "We're here to reflect and relax, not to be distracted by some time-wasting gizmo."

"Pooh-pooh," said Hubert. "For your information, I'm reading the Theme Farm show schedule for today."

I grabbed his tablet and spun it around toward me. *Today at Theme Farm* read the heading of the park's timetable.

"You clicked away before I could see what you were reading, didn't you?"

Hubert smiled smugly. "I'll never tell."

The tram pulled up to the main gate, to the sound of lively music. As Hubert and I stepped out, we were immediately greeted by a walk-around character: *Farmer Ward*—a cartoon version of the old man who conceived the park. It had been built on farmland that once belonged to him. A red barn, a tall grain silo, and a yellow farmhouse still stand as reminders. An old windmill towers over the park's central plaza, like a country version of the Eiffel Tower.

"Howdy, folks," said the cartoon farmer, wearing overalls and a straw hat on its *human* head. Having human heads on cartoon characters is a distinctive feature of Theme Farm, unlike other theme parks where characters are typically animals. That's because the whole place is run by *Fritterz*.

I guess I should explain that.

Fritterz—short for "freaky critters"—are the half -animal/half-human creatures that built, and now run Theme Farm. They owe their existence to a group of scientists, who were experimenting with cloning farm animals. The questionable ethics behind these tests stirred up public controversy, and the program was soon banned on moral grounds. But laboratory testing continued in secret, and went on for years afterwards.

Eventually, the illegal research proved too costly to maintain. The operation was about to be shut down, when by accident, some human DNA got into the cloning mix. The result was a freakish creature, that had never before walked this earth: a perfectly formed human with the head of a sheep!

The cloning technique was perfected to the point where scientists could clone humans with the head of any animal they chose. These creatures behaved like normal human beings, while retaining the skills their animal instincts provided naturally. Over time, an entire army of Fritterz were mass-produced, with the objective of using them as slave labor in manufacturing.

Federal agents later uncovered the acts of these

mad scientists and arrested them. The Fritterz were released from captivity, and cast into a world completely foreign to them. They were eventually accepted into society, but not without experiencing the same prejudice felt by any other minority. Passage of the *Fritter Rights Act,* however, changed all that, granting Fritterz the same rights as humans. Now with the freedom to speak out, they longed to offer their unique perspective on the human world. They figured the best way to do that was through a theme park, where people could come to enjoy themselves and benefit from their insights at the same time.

Now, how do I explain Theme Farm?

Like other theme parks, Theme Farm has rides and attractions, with plenty of food, fun, and frivolity for the whole family. People flock to these parks because they are places where dreams come true—something that hardly ever happens in real life. But the dreams that Theme Farm offers don't exist in a fantasy kingdom. The park's goal is to promote universal ideals like Peace, Justice, Equality, and all the other sadly lacking human virtues. For sure, Theme Farm has dancing fairies and singing pirates, but each one serves a purpose: to deliver an alternative worldview.

You would think this radical approach would

turn people off, but the concepts are so outlandish and fun that they keep coming back for more! A perfect example is a thrill ride that addresses an important environmental issue:

Flush Mountain. (You may get wet.)

Climb aboard a lilly pad vessel for a fairyland voyage, across a peaceful lake. Suddenly, the calm waters begin to swirl. Your boat spins as the water drops out beneath you. You plunge down a watery vortex, and find yourself speeding down a polluted river. A 50-foot drop over a yellow waterfall, and you settle onto a toxic lake. You try your best not to gag from the stench. Finally, you're sucked up into a giant vacuum cleaner, and emerge back into the serene setting where at all started.

"I don't want to miss the fireworks," said Hubert.

"When does it start," I asked.

He referred to his tablet. "A quarter to noon."

Theme Farm is also technologically more advanced than other parks. Fireworks in the middle of the day is a specialty. One whole section of the park had been built under an enormous, clear dome. Inside, any climate can be simulated from a spring rain to a violent thunder storm. The dome is actually made up of thousands of LCD panels that can be darkened to turn day into night. No more waiting for sundown to see a spectacular fireworks display.

There are so many other fantastic adventures to explore that it's hard to name them all. Some of my favorites are:

Puppet's Court: Puppets "pull the strings" to expose human injustice.

Corporate Cleaners: Where Wall Street investors are "hung out to dry."

Spin Doctor Mugs: After a good spinning, you can't tell the truth from the lies.

"Suppose we grab a bite before we get started," said Hubert.

It's always a good idea to go on Theme Farm rides on a full stomach—and with good reason. At other theme parks, you sit in a small vehicle, and are pulled along a metal track for a 3-minute excursion. But at Theme Farm, you may not come out of a ride for hours. Sometimes it's planned, sometimes it isn't. It all hinges on whether or not you've grasped the whole point of the ride. Sometimes a rider is having such a good time that he simply doesn't want to get off. When this happens, pagers are provided to alert friends and family when you finally exit the ride. In extreme cases, guests have been instructed to come back the next day to pick up their loved ones. It's very convenient.

"What are your taste buds hungry for?" asked Hubert.

It was still the breakfast hour, so Hubert and I chose the *Illegal Alien*: a Mexican-themed restaurant.

We climbed a tall ladder over a rusted, metal wall (It's part of the charm of the place), and went inside. Taking our seats at a sun-baked picnic table, we looked over the menu selection, while maria-chis in dirty blue jeans played "Guantanamera."

"May I take your orders?" said a voice. We didn't see anyone. Then we looked over the edge of the table and found a short server with a *Chihuahua* head.

"Are you ready to order Señor? Señorita?" he asked, in broken English.

"I'll have the Green Card Eggs and Ham," I said, "with Day-Laborer fries."

"How do you want your eggs?"

"Over-the-wall easy."

"I'll have the Boarder Patrol Omelet," said Hubert, "with a glass of Migrant Worker orange juice, please."

The bug-eyed waiter tipped his sombrero, then scurried off to the kitchen.

Waiting for our breakfast to be served gave Hubert and I a chance to talk.

"So, how's the lawsuit going?" asked Hubert.

"It's not a lawsuit," I said. "I'm exercising my right to be emancipated from my parents. Lincoln emancipated the slaves. Why shouldn't I have the same privilege?"

"If I had my way, you could move in with my family, but my narrow-minded folks won't hear of it."

"That's okay. I'll figure something out. I've just got to get away from my family."

"*Running* away is a more accurate statement, wouldn't you say?"

"Whatever. All I know is that if I don't bust out of that prison they call a home, I'm gonna scream."

"You don't know what you're talking about. You're thinking of this thing like it's some kind of an escape, but it's not that at all. I have a theory." (Hubert has theories on everything.) "You're not running, so much as *searching*. You're on a quest to find the perfect family."

"What's wrong with that? Doesn't everybody deserve one?"

"Wake up, girl! That's a statistical impossibility. There's no such thing. You should spend less time looking for a place to run away to, and more time finding out where you *belong*."

Hubert picked up a salt shaker and placed it in front of me. "See this?" he said. "Some huge corporate entity extracted this salt from the sea, packaged it, distributed it, and now here it is on our table. But the salt be-e-elongs in the ocean."

I put the pepper shaker alongside the salt. "At least it has company," I said. "And anyway, they're on the table because they be-e-elong in my stomach."

"And *you* belong with the parents who raised you. You're problem is that you're looking for a salt-and-pepper solution to a complex problem. We are born into this world under circumstances we have no control over. We cannot choose where, when, or to whom we will make our grand entrance."

"How philosophical. I just want to get out while I still have my sanity."

"Too late for that. You're *already* crazy. You've got a good thing going, and you don't even know it."

"Not as good as the Cleavers."

"Who are they?"

"You know, the family on those *Leave It to Beaver* reruns."

"They're a fake TV family of the early '60s—an idealized version of life that never existed. The *real* '60s were nothing like that. And if you don't believe me, I know a place you can go to see for yourself."

Hubert displayed a Theme Farm guide map on his tablet. He tapped the screen and zoomed into an attraction. "Here it is," he said. *"Used-to-Be TV."*

"What's that?"

"A new attraction. It's where you go into a room and sit down in front of a TV. You turn it on, but instead of watching a broadcast channel, you watch history as it's happening."

"That doesn't make sense. How can you watch something as it happens when it already happened?

"Apparently, those genius Fritterz found a way

to capture live video signals from the past, and display them on TVs in the present. You can even talk to people in real time, like talking to a neighbor over a fence, except that you're here and he's in another century."

"That's pretty cool, but what makes you think I'd be interested?"

"They're now displaying a signal from 1963!"

That was all I needed to hear. Used-to-Be TV would be my next Theme Farm stop. The idea of looking in on the '60s intrigued me. Imagine talking to someone in the time of Beaver, Opie, and Fred Flintstone.

Just then our canine server brought out our meals. He lifted Hubert's plate high over his head. "Dee plate is hot, Señor," he said, as he carefully slid it onto the table. My plate was nearly twice the size of the little dog waiter, but he scooted it over to me like a pro.

"Enjoy, Señorita," he said, then bowed to us and left.

"Dig in," I said to Hubert. But instead of picking up his fork, he unscrewed the top of the salt shaker and began filling his water glass with salt.

"What are you doing now, Mr. Wizard?" I asked.

"Sending this salt back home—down the drain and into the ocean where it belongs."

"That's the screwiest thing I've ever heard."

"I agree. The chances of it making it that far are

a million-to-one—about the same odds you have in finding what *you're* looking for."

"Thanks for the encouragement, Hubert."

"You're welcome."

We ate our breakfasts.

Chapter 3

Used-to-Be TV

*T*he outside of the attraction resembled a roomy, ranch-style house—the ultimate dream home for the mid-century family. Planter boxes with yellow daisies hung below every window. A basketball hoop was mounted above an aluminum garage door. You could almost hear the sound of a dribbling basketball, and the laughter of Billy and Biff enjoying a little one-on-one.

Rusty wagon wheels leaned against a wrought iron mail box, with *Used-to-Be TV* stenciled on the side of it. Being a new Theme Farm attraction, I expected to see huge crowds clamoring to get inside, but there was hardly anyone in line. All the better for me. I was anxious to get to the heart of the attraction: chatting with a fellow curiosity seeker in 1963!

I ambled up the red brick walkway to the front door—and the magical world beyond it.

Once inside, I followed the other visitors through an exact re-creation of a typical, suburban household of that era. The living room decor included a flagstone fireplace, a Mediterranean-style coffee table, and comfy chairs with crocheted, doily arm covers. Maple end tables sat on either side of a green sofa. On one table stood a lamp in the shape of a genie bottle, with the biggest lamp shade I've ever seen. On the other was a circular, tobacco pipe rack—the exclusive property of the man-of-the-house.

Family photos in brass frames sat on top of a spinet piano. Sheet music was propped up on a music stand above the keys, with titles like "Puff, the Magic Dragon," "Blue Velvet," and "Chim Chim Cher-ee."

A console TV in the corner ran news footage that underscored the optimism of the times: John Glenn orbiting the Earth in his *Friendship 7* spacecraft; President Kennedy playing touch football on the White House lawn; smiling people lined up to join the Peace Corps.

All the while, easy-listening music of that decade played softly in the background. Bossa nova melodies with lush string arrangements made me yearn for that stress-free lifestyle. Oddly, the music would periodically be interrupted by the voice of a TV show director, calling out shots to his cameramen:

"Standby. Ready camera two. Take two!"

The tour continued past a wood-paneled rumpus room, with a pool table and Tiki bar. A transistor radio in a teenager's bedroom played pop tunes of the day, like "Fingertips" by Stevie Wonder and "Surfin' USA" by the Beach Boys.

Then came the housewife's domain: the kitchen. The round eyes of a wall-mounted Kit-cat clock followed me as I entered. The down-home scent of biscuits in the oven, and bacon in a frying pan filled the air. I couldn't help taking a deep whiff of that mouth-watering aroma. On a breakfast table sat a portable black and white TV, with metal rabbit ears sprouting out the top. It played classic TV commercials. One showed a husband scolding his wife for making bad-tasting coffee. Another featured virile cowboys on horseback, promoting the manliness of smoking cigarettes.

The director's voice was heard again:

"Push in on camera three. Cue talent."

Finally, I was ushered into an oversized garage. Hula hoops, croquet sets, and shuffle board pucks were mounted to the walls. Rows of theater seats faced a large, plate-glass window, with video monitors on each side. Behind the glass was a TV studio control booth. Engineers stared at a wall of black and white TV screens, while seated at a broadcast control console.

The TV crew were all animatronic, human figures.

The director's voice could still be heard calling out instructions.

"Fade in graphics."

A title card faded up onto the audience monitors: *Welcome to Used-to-Be TV.*

I found a seat, which wasn't hard to do, considering the small group that had come in with me. As the lights dimmed, our robotic director, wearing an intercom headset, swiveled around in his chair to face us.

"Welcome, couch potatoes," he said. "As you can see, I'm in the middle of directing a TV show. The lights are on and the cameras are in focus. The only thing missing is the action—and that's where *you* come in!"

"Roll film."

The monitors showed a brief presentation to prepare us for what we were about to experience:

You enter a giant movie set of a suburban residential street, typical of the early 1960s. There you will find four quaint, little cottages. Select one and go inside. Sit down on the couch, and a TV in front of you will come on automatically. The pictures you see will be from video cameras in various locations. One might be in a TV studio.

Another might be a surveillance camera. The people, places, and things you see may look a bit out of date, but you're not watching a videotape. The images are *live* from 1963! At the same time, cameras in your room will be transmitting *your* image to those same locations in the past. All you have to do is watch and relax. Talk to people you see, if you like. They will be able to hear and see you.

"Cut to booth."

"It's an experience you will not soon forget," said the director. "Savor the fashions of that bygone era. Marvel at the discoveries of fifty years ago. Make friends. But there is one limitation you need to be aware of. Here is someone to tell you about it."

"Roll tape."

The monitors switched to a cartoon. An animated character hopped onto the screen. It was a vacuum tube, like the ones that used to power old-time radios, but with a cartoon face, arms, and hands.

"Hello, time-travelers," said the bubbly character, in a high-pitched voice. "I'm *Vaccy*, the vacuum tube."

The scene cut to the inside of a Used-to-Be TV cottage, as Vaccy bounced on to the couch.

"While we all want you to have a good time," he said, "there's always a risk that revealing too much about the present might change things in the past. So, whenever you're about to say something that might alter history, you'll hear this:"

A short burst of a *bleeping* tone sounded.

"Let me show you how it works."

A city street scene appeared on the cottage TV. A man in the background had just purchased a hot dog from a street vendor. *Happy New Year 1963* was painted on the side of the vendor's cart.

"Excuse me, sir," said Vaccy, addressing the screen.

The man was about to take the first bite of his lunch, when he turned toward the animated character. He came closer.

"You talkin' to me?" he said, his face now filling the screen.

"Yes," said Vaccy, "and I have something to tell you. I am speaking to you from the year *(bleep)*, and *(bleep)* is the first *(bleep)* president of the United States."

"What's that ya say?" said the confused man.

"People in our time talk on *(bleep)* phones, and surf the inter*(bleep)*."

Vaccy then turned to the audience. "See folks? No harm, no foul." He turned back to our man-in-the-street. "So long, average person from the past."

"Hey!" said the man. "What's this all a—"

"Cut!"

The screen went black.

"That's all there is to it," said the director. "And now, Theme Farm invites you to step into the amazing world of . . . Used-to-Be TV."

Dramatic music swelled as an automatic garage door opened onto a huge sound stage. There was the charming, suburban neighborhood the director had told us about. Movie lights simulated a time of day just after sunset. Sound effects of chirping crickets made it feel like I was really outdoors. Street lamps illuminated the four cottages, each with lush front lawns, bordered by neatly-trimmed hedges. The smell of fresh-cut grass brought back memories of the city park adventures of my youth.

Only a handful of people were on the street, most of them coming out of the cottages. None were going in. I strolled up to the bay window of the first cottage, and cupped my eyes with my hands to see inside. It was vacant.

I knocked on the front door, then slowly stepped inside. "Anybody home?" I called out, just to be courteous, then locked the door behind me. I was in a cozy living room, surrounded by early 1960s furniture. The soft light of a hanging swag lamp lit up a sunburst clock on a wall, covered in retro-pattern wallpaper.

It was eerily quiet.

A plaid couch in the middle of the room faced a

vintage black and white TV. I sidestepped the coffee table and sat down on the couch. As the TV came on, the screen displayed an old-style TV test pattern, with the words *Please Stand By*. I adjusted the couch pillows to get comfortable, and waited to see what would happen next.

The flickering pattern faded out. A black and white image popped up an instant later. I was watching the video signal from a camera outside a TV store, aimed down a city sidewalk. A sign off to one side read *See yourself on TV!* Passersby could see their faces on a TV in the store's display window—a clever ruse to draw people inside. I watched with amazement as average folks, dressed in their '60s attire, paraded up and down the street. City busses and classic cars drove by in the background. But no street sounds were coming out of the TV. I checked to make sure the volume was turned up.

A lady with a shopping bag stopped and looked into the camera. "Hello!" I said to her, waving my hand. But the woman just wiped her nose with a handkerchief and walked away. Evidently, she had seen herself in the store window TV, and *not* me.

I moved on to the cottage next door. The TV came on and showed the view of a security camera at a used car lot. The camera was at a high angle, like it was mounted to the roof of the sales office. Customers milled about, kicking tires and slamming car doors.

I definitely wasn't going to meet anyone here.

The TV in the next cottage only showed the words *College Media Studies,* superimposed over another test pattern. Just for the heck of it, I waited to see if something else would happen.

Nothing did.

No wonder there were no lines for this attraction. For sure, spying on a world fifty years in the past was fascinating, but not being able to interact with anyone made it hard to stay put.

I tried the last cottage, hoping I would find someone to talk to. This time I saw the inside of a security office, most likely in a commercial building of some kind. The back wall was covered in white, acoustical tiles. A row of video monitors showed images from surveillance cameras around the premises: an empty parking lot, deserted hallways, an idle, factory assembly line. The only thing moving was the second hand on a large wall clock.

In the center of the frame sat an empty office chair.

A minute or two rolled by.

"Hello?" I said faintly.

Nothing.

The sunburst clock in the cottage had read 12:20 when I first came in. Now it read 12:45—the same hour showing on the clock in 1963. Staring at the static screen all that time had exhausted my patience.

I got up and started to leave, when I noticed a shadow move across the back wall of the security office. I rushed back to the couch.

"Is there someone there?" I shouted.

The shadow entered the frame again. It was the silhouette of a man.

"Hey!" I cried. "Over here!"

The man-shadow turned left and right, as if having heard a voice—*my* voice.

"I'm right here," I said. "Sit down in the chair so I can see you."

But the man just scratched his head and shrugged his shoulders. Then the shadow walked out of frame.

I waited to see if the dark phantom would reappear, but after another ten minutes, it looked like that was all I was going to get.

Wow! Did I just have a close encounter with someone in 1963? The very idea had my head spinning. I couldn't just leave it at that. Maybe if I came back the same time tomorrow, I thought, the man would return as well. It was worth a try, and with a little luck, I might just experience a real *face-to-face* encounter.

Chapter 4

Clifford

*D*ay or night, rain or shine, if you need something in a hurry—whether it be band-aids and coffee, or diapers and beer—you will usually find it at the 24-hour *Jiffy-Q*. It was easy to find, with its flashing *OPEN* sign, and the lottery jackpot numbers brightly displayed in the window. I needed a few supplies before setting off again for Used-to-be TV, and my second attempt to contact the mystery man from the past.

As I entered the all-hours market, I immediately headed for the food section. It might take hours for my shadowy friend to appear, so I figured I had better stock up for the long haul, just in case.

"Good morning, Amy," said Yuuki Yokimoto, the gray-haired store manager. Yuuki was the last man you would expect to see behind the counter of a convenience store. To the locals he was considered either the town genius, or the village idiot, depending on who you talked to. He had a Ph.D in Sociology, and had been awarded the highest honors in his field. His paper, *The Social Interactions of Primates*, was required reading for all students entering the Social Sciences. But accolades don't pay the bills, and there were no openings for intellectuals in a town like Shankstonville.

"Can I help you find anything?" asked Mr. Yokimoto.

"Just munchies today, Yuuki," I said. I picked up some fresh fruit from the health foods section, a box of chewy fiber bars, and some string cheese.

Plump hotdogs turned on a hot-roller grill, by the self-serve beverage counter.

"How fresh are these dogs?" I asked Yuuki.

"Very fresh," he said. "Just put them on yesterday."

Then came the snack rack. Jiffy Chips, Jiffy Snaps, Jiffy Noodles, Jiffy Jelly, and dozens of other *Jiffy* brand treats filled the shelves. The Jiffy-Q chain of convenience stores featured food products made by its parent company Jiffy Snax Industries.

I passed on the high-fructose goodies, but not on the sugary drink in the refrigerated case next to them. Jiffy Fizz Cola was my only compromise to an otherwise healthy selection. With its signature red can, the drink was especially popular in Shankstonville, since the company had chosen our town to manufacture its most famous product.

"That's it," I said to Yuuki, placing my stash on the counter.

"Free fortune cookies with every purchase today," said Yuuki.

He opened a jar filled with the oriental treats. I cracked one open, popped the cookie in my mouth, and read the fortune inside: *Endurance and persistence will be rewarded.* I opened another cookie: *To foretell the future, you must visit the past.*

"I seem to have picked fortunes written just for me," I said.

"This must be your lucky day," said Yuuki.

"With all my good luck, maybe I should buy a lotto ticket."

"Sorry, Amy. Gotta be eighteen. Anyway, the jackpot's only up to six million. Hardly worth the two-dollar investment."

I handed Yuuki the exact change as he bagged up my purchase. "Anything else?" he asked.

"Yes. Why does someone with your intelligence stay around a cow town like this?"

He breathed in deeply. "I love the smell of manure in the morning."

I had to ask!

No food or drink allowed read the sign above the entrance to Used-to-Be TV. One thing nice about being a female is that no one considers carrying a large bag over your shoulder unusual. It's just normal. I carried such a bag into the cottage I had visited the day before. It not only held my snacks, but also a yellow notepad, a pen, and Hubert's spare tablet computer that he was kind enough to lend me. It was his backup in case the batteries in his other tablet died—a major dilemma in Hubert's world.

It was 12 noon exactly as I sat down on the couch. The TV came on as it should, and sure enough, there was the same scene in 1963!

Hubert's tablet found the Theme Farm Wi-Fi signal and connected to it. I could now search the Web, watch videos, and be entertained while waiting for something to happen on the TV. But I didn't have to wait long, as the sound of a door opening came through the TV speaker.

"Hello!" I shouted. But no one appeared on the screen. I sat perfectly still, desperately hoping for a reply, watching and listening.

Then a far off voice said, "Is someone there?"

"Yes!" I shouted back. "Over here!"

A man's face slowly leaned into the corner of the frame.

"Who's that?" he asked, gazing at me with wonder in his eyes.

"Come closer," I said. "I want to talk to you."

A middle-aged gentleman moved to the center of the frame. "What *is* this?" he said.

"Don't be alarmed, sir. You're going to find this

hard to believe, but I'm talking to you from *(bleep)*. I'm at a theme park attraction called *(bleep)*."

"I can't understand what you are saying," said the man.

I quickly took out the pen and yellow pad from my bag, and wrote down what I was trying to say in big letters. I held it up to the screen for the man to read, but the screen went blank. The live feed came back as soon as I took it down. (Those Fritterz don't miss a trick!)

"Who are you?" asked the man.

"My name's Amy. I'm talking to you from . . . er . . . a long ways away. What's your name?"

The bewildered man eased into the office chair. "My name is Earl. Earl Anderson."

"Nice to meet you, Mr. Anderson. What's that room you're in?"

"This is the security office in the building where I work. I'm employed by the *(bleep)* company."

"Are you the security officer?"

"No. We don't have one. In all the years I've been here there hasn't been a single security breach. We have this equipment here to keep our insurance company off our back."

Just then another off-camera voice chimed in. "Who are you talking to?"

Earl looked off camera. "Come in here, honey," he said.

A woman entered the frame and stared at me for

a moment, then turned to Earl. "I told you not to fool with this video equipment," she said. "What program is this?"

"It's not a program," said Earl. "This is Amy." He put his arm around the woman. "Amy, this is my wife, Sarah."

"Pleased to meet you, ma'am," I said.

Sarah put her face up to the screen, looking left and right. "Is this girl somewhere else in the building?"

"This is going to sound ridiculous, honey," said Earl, "but I think she's in the future."

Despite the skepticism in his own voice, Earl had figured out—however unlikely—what was happening.

"Don't be silly," said Sarah. "You've picked up a broadcast of the *Twilight Zone,* that's all."

The woman reached her hand toward the screen. "Don't turn it off!" cried Earl, brushing her hand away. "I want to talk to her."

Sarah pulled up another chair and sat quietly beside her husband.

"Tell me about yourself, Amy," said Earl.

"Well, I'm 16 years old. I go to *(bleep)* high school, and I enjoy jazz and reading."

Sarah playfully slapped Earl on the knee and laughed.

"You're so right, Earl," she said. "This isn't the Twilight Zone, it's *Candid Camera.*" She pointed at me. "But you sure don't look like Alan Funt."

"Just a minute," said Earl. Then he called off camera again. "Cliff! Come in here. I want you to meet someone."

Into the frame walked a tall boy about my age, flicking a yo-yo from his wrist.

"What's this, Pop?" asked the boy, with eyes wide.

"Amy," Earl said to me, "this is our son, Clifford. He's 17." He shoved the boy closer to the screen. "Say hello to Amy, son."

The frightened boy put his arms up in front of his face, as if fending off a swarm of attacking mosquitoes.

What a trip! There was a teenager like me, living in an age of high-top sneakers and Roy Rogers lunch boxes. The boy didn't appear to share my enthusiasm, however, as he quickly moved behind his parents without saying a word.

"He's a little shy," said Earl apologetically. "Let me tell you about myself, then."

Between the censored words, I got a sense of their location. The name of the town was bleeped out, but it apparently wasn't far from where I lived. Earl occupied some high position in his company.

He rattled off more information that the attraction would not allow me to hear, but by then I wasn't listening anyway. My attention was fixed on Clifford. Behind his slicked-down hair and buttoned-down collar, he was an attractive-looking boy. His timidness was kind of refreshing. I liked that he wasn't putting on some phony front to impress me, or displaying some kind of fake masculinity, like most boys do. There was a sweetness about him. He had that vulnerability that made me want to reach out to him—like an abandoned kitten that you want to hold and cuddle.

When my attention returned to Earl, he and his wife were both standing.

"C'mon, Sarah," said Earl. "I think we'll leave these two alone to talk." Clifford's face went blank, as his yo-yo twirled at the end of its string.

Earl patted his son on the back. "Talk to the girl," he said, then walked out of frame.

"Be nice to this young lady," said Sarah.

"Okay," replied Clifford.

Then his mom kissed him on the cheek. I watched curiously. What most people would regard as a common, everyday show of affection, seemed extraordinary to me. I was so full of disdain for my own parents, that the sight of tenderness between parent and child was almost overwhelming. I put my hands to my face and felt my cheeks redden. My god, I thought to myself, there it is: the family I always wanted!

Sarah smiled at her son and tousled his unkempt hair, before the hand of Earl reached in and pulled her away.

Clifford sat down, holding his yo-yo in his lap.

"Hello, Amy," he said, as he wound the string of his toy.

"So, Cliff," I said, "what do you do for fun?"

"Oh, lots of things. I like comic books. *Batman, The Flash.* Don't go much for *Archie* and that stuff. The ads in the back are kinda boss, though. I just ordered a pair of x-ray glasses."

Clifford's speech and mannerisms enchanted me, even though he was coming off like—in the words of his generation—a *drip!* I wouldn't be surprised if he blew a chewing gum bubble next. Still, the longer he spoke, the more fascinated I became.

"I like to go to the movies," he went on. "I saw *The Nutty Professor* last week. Jerry Lewis is keen-o! And I saw *Beach Party* just yesterday. Have you seen it?"

"I know it well," I said, being a fan of '60s cult movies.

Clifford's face lit up. "Annette Funicello. She's so choice!"

"I agree. Too bad she came down with *(bleep)*, isn't it?"

"What?" Clifford dropped his yo-yo to the floor. "Something's happened to Annette?"

The attraction wouldn't let me answer him, and maybe it was just as well. Hearing about Annette's unfortunate affliction would have shattered his world. What right did I have to do that? The harsh realities of his decade would be upon him soon enough. There would be a hellish war, student protests, and street riots that would rob the innocence of his whole generation. He should enjoy the wonderful life he was blessed with while he could. He was Peter Pan, and I didn't want to see him grow up.

I wanted to know Clifford better. I wanted to be a part of his family, as if that was even possible. But how could we communicate when we get *bleeped* every time we say anything meaningful?

"Ya know," said Clifford, twiddling his thumbs, "you're kinda cute."

"You're kinda 'choice' yourself," I said.

Clifford looked away, embarrassed, but smiling.

"I don't know many girls," he said. "The ones at school all go for the football hero types. There are a few who like to stuff love letters in my locker, but they're just messin' with me. I don't even know who they are."

"You're lucky," I said. "I'd love to have a secret admirer. I turn off boys because I'm too honest. I could tell them what they want to hear, but I don't like playing games when it comes to relationships."

Then Clifford looked at me with a warmth in his eyes I had never experienced before. There was a sincerity in his gaze that leaped off the screen and into my heart.

I should have looked away the moment our eyes met.

But I didn't.

I should have turned off the TV right then.

But I didn't do that, either.

I was heading for trouble and I knew it, but the closeness I felt for Clifford was impossible to ignore. I wanted to believe that he was just across the street, and not fifty years in the past; that he was watching me through a window, and all I had to do was open it and invite him into my life.

Earl's voice suddenly called out, "We're going now, Cliff."

Clifford looked down, sadly. "Well, I guess I gotta cut out."

"Same time tomorrow?" I said, without hesitation.

"What do you mean?"

"Can you come back? I have so much to tell you about *(bleep)*."

A broad smile crossed Clifford's face. "Well . . . sure! Yeah!"

"See you then," I said.

Clifford picked up his yo-yo, waved to me, then walked off.

A graphic popped up onto the screen: *Thanks for visiting Used-to-Be TV*. I walked out of the cottage into the make-believe neighborhood, then exited the attraction.

I shaded my eyes from the bright sunlight. I was outdoors, and surrounded by the sights, sounds, and smells of my own time. I felt like I had just awaken from a dream. Did I? The fact was that I had talked to a flickering image, no more real than the lines on a TV tube. I touched the bark of a nearby tree, and felt the summer breeze on my face. This was a reality I could *feel*. I had to wonder: did I really meet someone in 1963, or was this all some incredible illusion fabricated by Theme Farm?

Chapter 5

Pro Bono

Wallace, Evans, and Phillips, Attorneys at Law read the name on the office building directory. The shiny elevator doors parted, and I stepped inside. The smell of cafe mocha filled the roomy elevator car. After sharing my ride with men holding briefcases, and women with painted fingernails, I got off on the 16th floor. Down a long corridor was suite 1632: my destination.

I turned the brass door knob and entered the law office where Judge Higgins had sent me. The walls were covered with beveled wood paneling that seemed to glow under the amber lighting. Leather arm chairs lined the perimeter. In the center of the room were two back-to-back Chesterfield sofas, with buttons so deep you could get lost in them. It was stately and elegant—and agonizingly quiet. I didn't feel comfortable there. While the rich decor gave the room a warm feeling, there was a staleness in the air.

A large painting of Abraham Lincoln hung above the reception desk. The eyes of our 16th president seemed to follow me as I walked up to the receptionist.

"Excuse me, ma'am," I said to the young lady.

She was gazing at herself in a hand mirror. "Do you have an appointment?" she asked, chewing gum and examining the reflection of the tattoo on her neck.

"Yes," I said, "with Mr. Phillips."

A nose ring gripped her left nostril—not a very professional look for a place of business.

"Take a seat, and we'll call you," she said, never once looking up at me.

A number of men and women sat quietly in the plush waiting area. No one smiled. No one made eye-contact with me. I sat down among them and thumbed through a magazine. The tick-tock of a grandfather clock in the corner only accentuated the brutal silence. Was I in a law office, or a funeral parlor?

Behind the reception desk were three glass doors, exquisitely etched, in hardwood frames. A man in a stylish business suit came out of the first door, and greeted the woman sitting next to me. She began to weep the instant the man offered his hand to her. "I'm so sorry," he said solemnly, then escorted the grief-stricken woman, her head buried in her hands, to his office.

He was Mr. Wallace.

Out through the second door walked a rather portly gentleman, who approached the man sitting on the other side of me. The stout attorney stood over his client with a stern expression, his lips concealed under a bushy mustache.

Suddenly, a big-toothed grin appeared. "We've won!" he said to the man. They both laughed and slapped each other on the back as they retreated to his office.

He was Mr. Evans.

Then the last door opened. "Amy Dawson?" called out an elderly, white-haired man, in a cream-colored suit.

I raised my hand. "That's me."

The man waved me toward him. "Come this way, please," he said.

He stood in the office doorway, gazing at a legal document he held in his hand. As I squeezed past him, expecting a *"How are you,"* or a *"Nice to meet you,"* he just stared at the paper like I wasn't even there.

He was Robert Phillips—my attorney.

"Please sit down," said the wiry gentleman. He motioned toward a large oak desk with two chairs in front of it, each stacked high with papers.

"Here?" I asked.

"Oh, sorry," said Mr. Phillips. He tucked his paper under his arm and lifted a pile of documents from one chair. Stumbling across the cluttered office, he searched for somewhere else to put them, but every horizontal space was already taken. He kicked over a wastebasket before finally placing them on his desk, already littered with other documents.

The bumbling attorney sat down behind his desk, put on a pair of reading glasses, and resumed studying his paper. I craned my neck to see what he was reading, and recognized it as the petition I had filed with the court.

A long silence followed.

Glancing around his office, I saw framed parchment certificates on the walls, alongside diplomas from distinguished colleges and universities.

"Must have cost you a fortune in tuition," I said.

"Beg your pardon?" said the self-absorbed attorney, his paper never leaving his sight.

I sighed. "They said you were retired."

"I am."

"Then why are you still with this law firm?"

His lips moved as he continued reading his document. I guess his mouth was too busy to give me an answer.

A photo in a tabletop frame sat on the corner of his desk. I turned it around to get a look at it. The picture showed a much younger Mr. Phillips and an attractive young girl, with Mount Rushmore in the background.

My nosiness finally got me noticed.

"Please don't touch that," said the peeved attorney, peering at me over the top of his glasses.

"Who is the girl with you in this picture?"

"None of your business. And if you don't mind, keep your hands to yourself. I'll be with you in a minute."

I rotated the photo back into place.

What a grouch!

Finally, Mr. Robert Phillips—university graduate and former law professor—decided I was worthy of his attention. He set down the document, then leaned back in his squeaky, executive chair.

"Well, Amy," he said, "why are you here?"

"Can't you read?" I said. "It's all in that paper you've been gawking at for the last half-hour."

"I want you to tell me about it in your own words."

"I'm divorcing my parents. Okay?" I held up my petition. "It's all spelled out right here."

"This document only tells me of your intentions. It doesn't tell me why."

"Excuse me . . . *Bob*. I don't wish to sound rude, but are you an attorney or a shrink? Judge Higgins said you could get all this legal crap settled. Are you going to help me or not?"

"You seem a little upset."

My fingers clenched into fists. "That's it! I'm leaving!" I got up from my chair and stormed toward the office door.

Then out of the blue, Bob asked, "Are you happy?"

I turned back around and narrowed my eyes at him. "What did you say?"

"I asked if you were happy."

I marched back to his desk and pointed at my own angry face. "Do I look happy to you?"

Bob leaned forward in his chair, then dug a file folder out from under the clutter of his disheveled desk. "Okay," he said. "That's all I wanted to know." He opened the folder, revealing the documents inside. "Sign these papers, and you can go. I'll messenger them back to Judge Higgins and you'll have no trouble settling your case."

The papers were prepared with red-arrow stickers by the dotted lines that awaited my signature. Bob handed me a pen.

Finally, some action!

I grabbed the pen and started to sign the first page, but as I pressed the pen to the paper, I froze. The finality of the situation hit me with full force. This was it! My signature would mean that separating from my family was as good as done.

My hand started to shake. I slowly raised my head up to look at Bob. "I have a confession to make," I said meekly.

"Yes?"

"I'm . . . I'm afraid."

"It's a scary thing, dissolving a family," said Bob. "All the things you went through together; the ups, the downs; the triumphs and the failures; the laughter and the tears—all wiped away with the stroke of a pen."

I hung my head. A teardrop blotted the very paper that was meant to bring me happiness.

"Please, help me," I said, like a little lost lamb crying for its mother. "I don't know what I should do."

Mr. Phillips slowly withdrew the pen from my fingers.

"I think you'd better sit down, Amy," he said.

I slumped back into my chair as Bob placed a box of tissues within my reach.

"You're a gutsy young lady," he said. "It takes a lot of courage to do what you're doing, and I commend you for it. But a commitment like this can't be made in good conscience until you understand the risks."

"I'll risk everything if I have to," I said. "There's got to be another family out there who I can relate to."

"Okay. Suppose you find such a family. Let's assume they're the nicest, most caring group of people on the planet. You have everything you need, and you're as happy as you can be. But having left your *own* family, in itself, can be problematic."

"What problem? You've just described the perfect solution."

"Not quite. Emancipation carries a stigma. Your friends at school find out what you've done, and they stop talking to you. The other kids make rude remarks behind your back. You can try to keep it in the background, but with social media the way it is, there's not much chance of that happening."

My sister would gladly lead the charge on that front. One text message to her band of gossipmongers and I'd be toast.

"And what about when it's time to enter the workforce?" continued Bob. "When employers discover your family history, you'll be labeled as unstable, reckless, and unreliable.

Bob picked up the phone on his desk and punched in a number, then said into the receiver, "Will you come in here for a moment, please?"

The office door opened, and in came the receptionist, smacking her gum-laden jaws. She crossed her arms and tilted her head to one side as if to say, *"Why are you bothering me?"*

"You wanted to see me, boss?" she asked.

"Yes," said Bob. "Will you set up an account for Amy? You'll need to create the usual data files, enter her contact information, and all that."

She turned and left the room without so much as a *"Yes, sir."*

"Now, tell me, Amy," said Bob, "what are your impressions of her?"

"That's easy," I said. "Self-centered, uneducated, and lazy."

"You left out suffering from depression and low self-esteem. It so happens that young lady has a degree in Economics. She does all of our billing and database management, and handles our book-keeping, too. Her people skills need some work, obviously, but she's a good worker. She was passed over by every employer in town because she lived in a foster home. The facts of her disadvantaged past will always be an obstacle for her."

I wanted to crawl under a rock. My assessment of that girl was way off. And after hearing about the horrendous abuse she had suffered at home, *my* situation suddenly didn't seem so bad.

"Leaving your family can also create problems in personal relationships," said Bob. "Finding a boyfriend won't be easy. Your tarnished reputation will be *his*, too. And if you're already in a relationship, you'd better tell him what you're up to."

I wasn't prepared to bring up my strange encounter with Clifford. We were far from being in a relationship, but lying to him about my family problems wouldn't be easy for me.

"Actually," I said, "I do know someone who might treat me differently if he knew about this.

He's not a boy friend, but he's someone I care about. You can't really maintain a relationship with someone who lives in 1963."

Bob gave me a funny look. "I don't think I follow you."

"Well, you see, there's this attraction at a theme park that lets you talk to people in the past, through this crazy TV set. It's hard to explain. Anyway, that's where I met him."

"I think I know the attraction you mean. At Theme Farm, right? It's called Used-to-Be TV."

"Then you know that trying to build a relationship with someone is nearly impossible. All that bleeping!"

"What if I told you I know a workaround for that?"

I brightened. "You have . . . I mean . . . you do?"

He reached into his desk drawer and pulled out a business card, that looked like it had gone a few rounds with a washing machine. It read:

The Great Abra-ca-zebra
Magic for all ages
Parties, Banquets, Special Events

"He's a Fritter," said Bob. "Half-zebra. He was a client of mine. He was sued for setting a house on fire while doing a flaming, dove pan trick at a birthday party. He now works at the Theme Farm

Magic Shop. Go there and show him this. He's got more than just party tricks up his sleeve."

"You mean . . ?"

"He'll make your conversations *bleepless.*"

What a break! I could have kissed old Bob, but I was afraid it might be in breach of the attorney-client code.

Bob stood up and shook my hand.

"About your case," he said, "this is a big step you're taking. Think about what I've said, and we'll meet again. Okay?"

"Sure thing, Bob," I said. "By the way, do you mind if I don't call you Mr. Phillips? It sounds so formal."

"*Bob* is fine . . . Miss Dawson."

I started for the door, then turned back to Bob.

"You know," I said, "changing my mind about going ahead with this won't change how my parents feel about *me.*"

"You don't have to worry about them," said Bob. "They're having second thoughts, too."

"How do you know that?"

"I met with them yesterday, and they feel terrible about the whole thing. They're as much on the fence as you are."

I wish I could have believed him. Reconciling with my folks was not an option. After what they said about me in court, I knew there was no going back.

I walked up to the receptionist as I returned to the waiting area. She was entering my name into her computer, all the while chomping on her gum.

"Got anymore?" I asked.

"Anymore what?" she said.

"Gum."

She looked at me strangely. "Sure, kid," she said, then handed me a stick from her purse.

I stared at the pierced and tattooed young woman. She still had a snippy edge to her, but I was able to look beyond that now. It just shows how wrong it is to judge people, before you see what's behind the war paint.

"What are *you* looking at," she grumbled to me.

I just smiled. "Thanks for the gum," I said, then saluted Abe Lincoln on my way out.

Chapter 6

Clicker

When I was a little girl, my grandfather showed me a magic trick. It went like this:

He placed a coin in his hand, then closed his fingers around it. When he opened his hand for me to retrieve it, the coin was gone!

"Where did it go?" I asked, a perfectly reasonable question for a 6-year-old.

He reached behind my ear with his other hand and, low and behold, there was the coin!

Amazing! I was so impressed. I laughed, and asked the customary followup question: "How did you do that?"

Granddad showed me how the trick was done. He had palmed the coin in one hand, while pretending to place it in the other. The hand that I thought held the coin was empty the whole time. The naïve girl that I was, it never occurred to me that he would tell me one thing, then do another.

It was a simple magician's trick that had fooled little ones like me for centuries. Granddad was only trying to entertain me, but I saw it as a betrayal of my trust. A lie. Most kids would have marveled at his cleverness, but not me. I was weird that way.

A shame, too. I so wanted to believe in magic. I was at that age when fairy tales came true; when true-love's kiss awakened the sleeping beauty inside us all.

And so I walked in to the Theme Farm Magic Shop with a head full of disbelief.

It was a small store, with rings for linking, silks for vanishing, and hats for pulling rabbits out of. It was kind of dark and gloomy inside, almost medieval in style, which might have explained why there were no shoppers.

Behind a tall counter stood a magician, or so I assumed—he wore a turban. I knew he was the Fritter I was looking for. His turban sat atop a zebra head.

The striped magician stared at me as I approached the counter. His piercing, dark eyes followed my every step.

"Good morning, sir," I said politely. "I wonder if you can tell me—"

"Silence!" he suddenly blurted out. "Speak no more, for I know why you have come. You seek the wisdom of the ancient mystics."

"Not really," I said. "I was sent here to—"

"To learn the forbidden secrets of the Wizards of Tantagria."

Then he raised his black cape above his head like Dracula. A strobe light flashed. Thunder rolled out of a hidden subwoofer. What drama!

"Do you want to hear what I have to say," I said, "or are you going to keep interrupting me?"

A long, white cane popped out into the air. The zebra grabbed hold of it in a grand flourish.

"Come hither, ye seeker of knowledge, and I shall grant thee audience." Then he tapped me on the shoulder with the cane, like King Arthur knighting Sir Lancelot.

I applauded him.

"You can put your tricks away now, Blackstone," I said. "I just want to ask you a question."

The comical zebra collapsed his cane back into a palm-sized roll, then looked at me, puzzled. "Aren't you amazed?"

"Most entertaining," I said, "but those old tricks don't do anything for me."

He removed his turban, revealing his pointy zebra ears. "No point in performing for nothing." Then he untied his cape and neatly stowed it under the counter.

"I will admit," I said, "your presentation is very cool. Your routine is kinda cute."

"Cute?" said the offended zebra. "I'll have you

know, young lady, that thousands once flocked to see me perform astounding feats of magic. I amazed crowds the world over with illusions no one could figure out." He turned his head and scanned the store. "Now look at me—in a theme park magic shop. It's not fair!"

He brushed his stiff mane with the palm of his hand, then adjusted his black bow tie in a mirror on the wall. "Now, what did you want to see me about, young maiden?"

"I was sent here by an old friend of yours," I said. "Robert Phillips. He's an attorney."

"Don't know anyone by that name," he said. "And I don't socialize with anyone in the law profession, especially attorneys! They're the only humans who can deplete your dignity and your bank account at the same time."

"You know him," I said. "You just forgot."

I placed the business card Bob had given me on the counter.

The zebra's eyes widened as he picked up the card, recognizing it as his own.

"Where did you get this?" he asked.

"From the man you claim not to know."

The zebra was fuming. His eyes were on fire as he stared at the card. Then he pointed to the front door.

"Get out of here!" he said firmly.

"Not without some answers!" I said.

"Leave the premises at once before I call security to have you dragged out."

I stood firm. We stared at each other intensely. Then I held the business card up to his face.

"Are you *The Great Abra-ca-zebra?*" I asked.

The defeated magician's ears lowered as a great sadness filled his eyes.

"Was," he said softly.

Apparently, showing him the card had forced him to recall a past that he did not want to revisit. I felt bad about that. But the secret to Used-to-Be TV was locked in his brain, and I wanted the key to open it.

"My failed past is my eternal curse," said the zebra. "It's not your fault."

He reached his hand out to me. "Call me Zeb."

I shook his hand. "Call me Amy."

Just then a young boy with a bright red, mohawk haircut strolled into the shop. He wore a black leather jacket with an insignia on the back. *Dante's Magic Society* was written above an embroidered picture of a human skull, with lightening bolts shooting out of its eye sockets. He couldn't have been more than twelve.

The boy swaggered up to the counter, like he was the head of a motorcycle gang.

"Hey you, zebra man!" said the cocky juvenile. "You got any Mystery Smoke?"

Zeb looked down at him. "Whatever are you

talking about, my little maggot?"

"You know, the stuff you rub on your hands and smoke comes off your fingertips. It comes in a little, white tube."

"Are you a magician?"

The boy turned and pointed to the insignia on his jacket. "Don't diss me, you striped jackass. I've got the *Rule The World* magic set, the *Make Fools of Your Friends* kit, and the *Magicians Get The Girls* instruction book."

"You don't need smoke," said Zeb. "You need someone to hose you down." Then he leaned over the counter and squirted water in the boy's face from a fake carnation on his lapel.

The boy opened his jacket, and a white dove flew out. The bird circled the shop, then passed over Zeb's head, where it deposited a smelly, white blob on his shoulder.

Zeb grabbed a plaster Wolf Man statue from the shelf behind him and took a swing at the dove, then threatened the boy with the heavy object.

"Be gone, you little savage!" shouted Zeb. "And take your infernal arrogance with you!"

The boy turned up his nose as the dove perched on his shoulder. Then they casually sauntered out of the shop together.

Zeb put away his Wolf Man weapon.

"I've seen it a thousand times," he told me, wiping the poo from his coat with a red magician's silk. "That '*I know the secret of magic, and that makes me better than you*' attitude. Frightful behavior for one so young. And where does he come off talking to me that way? I remember a time when the youth of this country showed respect for their elders."

"Like, back in . . . 1963?" I said.

Zeb looked at me suspiciously. "Why did you pick *that* year?"

"It's what I've been trying to ask you about. That's the year you tune in to at Used-to-be-TV."

Zeb tossed away his soiled silk and looked me in the eye. "What is it that you want to know?"

"I've been told that you can put a stop to the bleeping."

"Is that so? Well, maybe I can, and maybe I can't. Why do you want to?"

I was uncomfortable telling him about Clifford. I would be opening up my personal life to a total stranger. Confessions like that are usually shared between mothers and daughters. But since my mom and I weren't speaking, a magic zebra would have to do.

"I met someone on channel '63," I said.

"Define *met*."

"What I mean is, I've been talking to a boy, but there's all this bleeping, and . . . I think I *like* him."

The inquisitive zebra put his elbow on the counter, rested his head on his hand, then stared wistfully into my eyes. "How much?"

"A lot."

"*How,* a lot?"

His questioning was getting more personal by the moment, and I was starting to feel a little embarrassed.

"No need to answer, my dear," said Zeb. "I know that look. You're in love."

"That's not possible," I insisted.

"It's true, and don't ask me how I know. A magician never reveals his secrets."

"But we barely said anything to each other. I only talked to him a few minutes."

Zeb let out a laugh. "A few minutes? You have fifty years between the two of you, and you're worried about a few measly minutes? Stop watching the clock, Amy, and start following your heart. Tell this boy how you feel, and leave Time to the watchmakers."

"I'll feel foolish if I do."

"Only fools run from a chance at love. Used-to-Be TV was created to bring people together, not keep them apart."

"How do you know so much about it?"

Zeb placed a glass pitcher of milk on the counter, then rolled a newspaper into a cone. He poured the milk into the paper container, and when the pitcher was empty, he quickly unrolled the paper. I expected milk to splash all over me, but the newspaper was perfectly dry.

Then I noticed the headline: *Fritter Discovers Time Portal.* Zeb's face was pictured below it.

"You?" I said, pointing to the headline.

Zeb smiled and nodded.

"Now I *am* amazed," I said. "How did you come up with that?"

"I don't rightly know. Some bit of genius must have gotten into my DNA when I was cloned into a Fritter. I always enjoyed science and tinkering with electronics.

"Then one day it hit me, that space never changes; that the ground we stand on today is the same ground no matter where we are in Time. The problem is that we only get to experience that space in that fleeting moment called The Present. Video signals, once broadcast into the ionosphere, never completely disappear. So, I invented the *Time Transducer:* a device that intercepts those signals from long ago, and displays them for us to enjoy today. I later sold my concept to Theme Farm—and voila! Used-to-Be TV!"

"But why did you add all that bleeping?"

"To prevent anyone from tampering with history. Without it, how would we know that the world we see today wasn't shaped by someone fooling with the past? There are a lot of wicked people out there who would just love to abuse this power."

"Forget about those bad people," I said. "Think

of all the *good* you could do with something like this. You could reverse all the tragic events that happened in the past. Save lives. Maybe it wouldn't work every time, but at least you could try."

Zeb paused and stared up at the ceiling—his mind traveling to some other region.

"I *did* try," he said sadly. "In early testing I tuned the device to channel '64, and locked on to a video signal in the White House. Lyndon Johnson was president then. He was seated at his desk in the Oval Office when my face popped onto a TV screen in front of him. What if I told you that there was no Vietnam War?"

"Of course there was," I said. "It's in all the history books."

"*Now* it is. Johnson had only been in office a few weeks, and was mulling over what to do with the American troops that were already there. I told him that the Communists had overrun the country in the future. He wasn't happy to here that. But when I told him that Richard Nixon would defeat him in his reelection, he went ballistic."

"But Vietnam *was* taken by the Communists, and Nixon *did* become president. So you see, you didn't change history at all."

"Yes. But what I didn't know then was that Johnson was about to withdraw our military forces and be done with the whole mess. Instead, he escalated our involvement. His unpopularity from that decision forced him not to run for a 2nd term. Then came the draft, the protests, the riots. I tried to reestablish my connection with 1964, to dissuade Johnson from doing anything rash, but by then the signal was lost for good."

The zebra turned his back to me and reached for a metal flask he had hidden on the shelf. His head tilted back as he took a long swig from it.

"50,000 soldiers died from me interfering with history," said Zeb, returning the bottle to its hiding place. "That's a hell of a burden to carry. I sought to rid the world of hatred between nations, but I caused more hostility and death as a result." He reached out and took hold of my hand. "You, on the other hand, seek love—and maybe you'll find it in 1963."

Then Zeb waved his hand in the air and, seemingly out of nowhere, produced a small metal box with a single push-button on the top.

"What's that?" I asked, mystified.

"A clicker. Pressing this button will defeat the bleeping feature in the Time Transducer program."

Zeb reached out and offered it to me, but stopped short of placing the device in my hand.

"I wasn't really a world-class magician like I told you," he confessed. "I worked in a traveling circus as a sideshow freak: *The Amazing Zebra-headed Man.* Many Fritterz made their living that way, before the Fritter Rights Act. Traveling the world as a famous magician was a dream that never saw the light of day. Performing at birthday parties and working in this ridiculous shop was as close as I got to it."

"What about the Time Transducer?" I said. "That's magic if I ever saw it."

Zeb looked closely at the clicker. "I was going to destroy this thing, with all the grief it has caused. But I give it to you with all my heart, with the prayer that you will use my invention for which it was created."

He handed me the device, then suddenly clasped his fingers around my hand. "But be warned," he said sternly. "Watch what you say. One wrong word and history as we know it will be changed forever."

"I'll be careful."

"I know you will. You're a brave and intelligent girl, and you now know that the past isn't something to be toyed with. But that's not what I'm really worried about."

"Why? What else can go wrong?"

"There are consequences to finding love on Used-to-Be TV. Love is a magical thing, but it can cause more pain than you can imagine. Take what you will from this relationship with this boy. Share your thoughts, express your feelings, but let it go no further than that. Remember, you may make a deep, emotional connection with him, but there will be no physical bonding. You may find his companionship comforting, but you will never hold his hand. Keep his memory in your heart, but come back to the present. Embrace today, for you cannot touch the past."

I appreciated Zeb's concern, and heeded his warning. But as I took hold of the magic clicker, all I could think about was running over to Used-to-Be TV to have a real conversation with Clifford.

It occurred to me that the clicker might not be for real. Maybe it was just an empty box with a switch on top. I was in Theme Farm, after all, where nothing is what it seems. The Great Abra-ca-zebra might have been using slight-of-hand to fool me—like my grandfather had done so many years before.

I hoped that wasn't so. This was no time for deception. My fondness for Clifford was beginning to make me believe in magic all over again.

Chapter 7

Uncensored

*T*he TV was on.

The volume was up.

I sat on the couch and stared at the empty office chair in 1963. Nothing had changed on the Used-to-Be TV screen from what I saw the day before, except for the wall clock. It read 12:23—the exact time when I last spoke to Clifford.

I set my can of Jiffy Fizz Cola down on the coffee table, under a Jiffy-Q beverage coaster. Mr. Yokimoto was giving them away as part of the store's *Family Fun Month* promotion.

The clock clicked over to 12:24.

"Cliff?" I said, to the TV screen. "Are you there?"

"Coming!" said the far-off voice of Clifford—my teenage counterpart fifty years in the past.

He walked into frame, carrying an old-style briefcase, then plopped down in his chair.

"Hi, Amy," he said. Then he opened his case and

pulled out an old *Instamatic* camera and put it up to his eye. A second later, its F*lash Cube* went off.

"Hey!" I said. "What was that for? You didn't even give me time to smile."

"You were fine," he said. "I wanted to capture this moment in pictures. It's our first meeting together without a chaperone."

"Yeah, okay. But maybe we should get better acquainted before we start setting up a photo gallery. For starters, where are you?"

Instead of answering me, he stepped out of frame, returning a moment later with a tall glass of water. He took a jar out of his briefcase, scooped a teaspoonful of an orange, powdery substance from it, and stirred it into the water with a spoon.

"Sorry about this," he said, "I didn't have time to grab breakfast this morning."

"What is that?" I asked.

"*Tang.* It's what the astronauts drink. John Glenn drank it when he orbited the Earth. It gives you that extra boost of Vitamin C."

"Do they still make that stuff? I've never seen it at the *(bleep)*."

That blasted bleeping! It was time to test out the magic clicker. Either I was going to be free of that annoying sound, or I would learn that Zeb, the magic zebra, was really a fraud.

While Clifford chugged down his space drink, I took the clicker from my bag, pointed it at the screen, and pushed the button. I heard a high-pitched *ping*. That was all. I didn't see any change in the picture.

"What was that you said?" asked Clifford, wiping the powdery drink from his upper lip.

"I said, I've never seen Tang at the . . . *Jiffy-Q.*"

No bleeping!

It worked!

"The Jiffy what?" asked Clifford.

Uh, oh! Only seconds had passed since I turned off that bothersome bleeping, and already I was revealing information about the future. I had divulged the existence of Jiffy-Q to someone in a time before convenience stores. Still, I only mentioned it in passing. How much damage could that do?

"I've never heard of a Jiffy-Q," said Clifford. "Do they give Green Stamps?"

"It's just a store near where I live," I said, making light of my remark.

"Well, if they don't carry Tang, they're missing out. It's one of America's most popular drinks."

I reached down and held up my Jiffy Fizz Cola. Its iconic red cans were known the world over, and I was well aware that it existed in Clifford's time.

"More popular than *this?*" I said, holding the can alongside my face.

"Nothing's more popular than that," he said, "and I should know."

Clifford dug into his case again, this time coming up with a copy of *Big Business Magazine,* from the year 1951. The edges were worn, and the loose pages were ready to fall out. The cover read *Jiffy Snax Industries' Bold Move,* above a closeup of its trademark can. Then he flipped to the cover story inside. It showed a picture of a Jiffy Fizz Cola bottling plant, with a *Grand Opening* banner above the main entrance. Company representatives and local officials posed in front of the building. One of them held a small child in his arms.

"*This* is where I am," said Clifford, "in the Jiffy Fizz building."

I knew the building well. The Jiffy Fizz Bottling and Distribution Center was the largest structure in Shankstonville. Huge trucks with the Jiffy Fizz logo were a common sight on the Interstate exit into town.

"I'm the little kid in this picture," said Clifford, "and that's my dad holding me. He used to bring me around to show me the construction progress. I scratched my initials in some wet cement by the front entrance once when he wasn't looking. Boy, did I get it for that one! I felt so bad that I wrote a letter of apology and stuffed it in a gap in the bricks just above it. But when they made my dad Head of Marketing, all that was forgotten. That's how we ended up moving to *Dorian.*"

Shankstonville had originally been named

Dorian back in 1899, for the Spanish missionary Father Dorian, who settled there. The name was changed in the 1920s, after our beloved founding father was caught bootlegging whiskey during Prohibition.

Clifford squinted his eyes at me. "I think there's something wrong with your Jiffy Fizz can," he said. "The design doesn't look right."

"That's because it was made in the year . . . in the year . . ."

"What is it, Amy? What are you trying to say?"

"You'd better put down your Tang, Cliff. You're not going to believe what I'm about to tell you. I'm talking to you from the future—fifty years ahead of your time, to be exact."

"Naw," said Clifford. "You're pulling my leg. You're in some other part of the building . . . aren't you?"

I took out Hubert's tablet and held it up to the TV. "Ever seen one of these?" I asked Clifford, hitting the device's video record button.

"Sure I have. It's a baseball card binder," he said.

I flipped the tablet around to let Clifford see its display, then hit the playback button.

Sure I have. It's a baseball card binder.

"Golly!" said Clifford. "That's pretty nifty. How did you do that?"

I heard the echoes of 6-year-old Amy, asking for the secret to my grandfather's vanishing coin trick. To Clifford, what I had shown him was no less magical. But this was a secret I didn't dare give away. I had given Clifford a demonstration of future technology, and might have already altered history in doing so.

I checked out the tablet—front to back, top to bottom, side to side. It hadn't changed in the slightest. Video capturing Clifford was a risky move, but it was the only way I knew to show him that I was telling the truth.

"What you're saying is pretty hard to swallow," said Clifford. "Now I want to ask *you* a question."

Here it comes, I thought. Now he'll want to know all about the world of the future, that I promised I wouldn't reveal to anyone.

I put my Jiffy Fizz down on the coffee table. "Okay. I'm ready."

"What's your favorite color?"

Whew! I was off the hook for now.

"Blue," I said, "like the blue streak in the back of my hair." I turned my head to show him. "See?"

"I'll have to take your word for that. I can only see black and white in these monitors." He held up the magazine showing the can of Jiffy Fizz Cola on the cover. "Personally, I'm partial to the color red."

"Yuck! Your dad could due with a lesson in Marketing. Those cans should be blue. You know?

The deep *blue* ocean? The clear *blue* sky? Blue says, refreshment!"

"Hm. That's a very interesting point."

I grabbed my drink to take another sip. I brought it up to my lips, not giving it another thought, until I crossed my eyes and looked at the can.

It was *BLUE!*

Now I had really done it! I had abused the power of the Time Transducer with my big mouth, and it was too late to change it back.

"I'll pass your suggestion on to Dad," said Clifford.

"I think you already did," I said.

"What?"

"Never mind."

I immediately changed the subject. "So, tell me what it's like to be a teenager in 1963?"

"Uh, uh," said Clifford. "You go first. What's a typical day like for Amy of the future?"

"Not much different from yours, I imagine. I go to school, take out the trash, and quarrel with my siblings."

"I don't have any siblings—not so far, anyway."

"Be glad you're an only child. Believe me, it makes life a lot simpler. Now, it's your turn."

Clifford dove into his briefcase once again.

"Since we're trapped in this time tunnel," he said, "suppose we go even further back in time." He produced a photo album with the words *Our Clifford* on the front cover. A photo record of his whole life from day one was inside, thanks to his foresighted parents.

He held the album up to the TV screen and opened it. "We'll skip the early ones," he said.

"No, no!" I said. "I want to see your baby pictures."

"I'd rather you didn't. You'll see my naked fanny."

"All baby pictures are that way."

"Really? Is yours?"

I thought for a moment, but couldn't recall how mine looked. There were plenty of photos of me growing up, but none of me as an infant, that I could remember.

"Have it your way," I said. "I'll just search them online and see them anyway."

"What's *online* mean?" he asked.

"You were going to show me your pictures, remember?" I said, skirting his question.

He thumbed ahead to a picture of a young Clifford, standing next to a man in a Buck Rogers-style spacesuit. The man wore a spherical, glass helmet on his head, with two little antennas sticking out the top.

"That's me at Disneyland when I was eight," said Clifford. "I wanted my picture with Davy Crocket, but my folks thought he was too violent of a role model for me."

"I agree with them," I said. "Seeing all that gunplay isn't healthy for a developing brain."

Then he stopped at a photo of him seated at an old, upright piano. "My folks started me on piano lessons when I was nine. I still play. I write songs, too."

"You do?" I said, intrigued. "Can I hear one?"

Clifford's shyness quickly re-surfaced. "Well, maybe someday."

The remaining photos included him clowning in the stands at a high school football game, and playing Curly in a local production of *Oklahoma!*

His most up-to-date photo was of him dancing on the *American Bandstand* TV show. One showed him actually shaking hands with Dick Clark, the show's iconic host. My first impression of Clifford may have been wrong. The boy I pegged as an introverted dweeb, was more outgoing than I thought.

"I first went out to Hollywood with my music class," explained Clifford. "I've been there one other time since. It's cool. I'd love to take you there."

I was so taken with Clifford's enthusiasm that I forgot about the one thing we couldn't do. No matter how engaging, or intimate our conversation, we could never meet in person.

"Oh, sorry," moaned Clifford, realizing what he had said.

There was a long silence.

"Well, Amy," said Clifford, his head bowed. "I guess I should get going. I'm meeting my parents for lunch at The International House of Fondue."

"Same time tomorrow?" I said.

Clifford looked up at me, smiling. "You mean it?"

"Of course, dummy. You're not going to get rid of me that easy."

With all the constraints that time-twisting contraption wedged between us, I was still having the time of my life. Clifford was more than just a face on a TV screen. With all the personal problems I was having to deal with, he was the light in my hour of darkness.

"One more thing before you leave," I said. "Bring your face closer." Clifford leaned in. I aimed my tablet at him, then positioned myself next to the TV set. I smiled and snapped a picture.

"What was all that?" asked Clifford.

"It's a selfie, for my *own* album."

"It's a what?"

"A story for another day. Bye!"

I stopped by the Magic Shop on my way out of Theme Farm. Zeb had given me an awesome gift, and I wanted to thank him for it.

As I walked into the shop, a different Fritter was standing behind the counter, this one with the head of an Angora rabbit.

"I'm looking for Zeb," I told the furry salesclerk.

"Who did you say?" he asked.

"Zeb. The Great Abra-ca-zebra."

"No one here by that name."

"But I saw him here."

A fox-headed man stepped up behind the rabbit. "Can I help you, young lady?" he said. "I'm the manager."

"Yes. Don't you even know who works in your own store?"

"I know *everybody* who works here."

"Then where's Zeb, the zebra? He stood right where you're standing just yesterday."

"No one named Zeb, and no zebras, have ever worked here. And whomever you think you saw, it must have been somewhere else. We've been closed all week for remodeling. Just opened back up this morning."

"That's impossible! He gave me this." I pulled the magic clicker out of my bag.

"Oh, we sell those," said the fox. He reached under the counter and pulled out a clicker exactly like mine. He handed it to me, and when I pushed the button I got an electric shock so intense that I dropped the devilish thing to the floor.

The fox and the rabbit shared a good laugh at my expense.

"That's one of our best-selling gags," said the

fox, between chuckles.

I picked up the evil novelty and threw it back at them. "You think this is funny, playing a joke on a complete stranger?"

"If anyone's playing a joke," said the fox, "I'd say it was your zebra friend. He sold you a defective product." The fox reached out to take my clicker. "Here, I'll get you a new one."

I held my precious device close to my chest. "Not on your life!" I said, then ran out of the shop as fast as I could.

Chapter 8

Endangered

*T*he name of the ride was *Searchin' Safari*. Join a mind-bending expedition in search of the absurdities in human behavior.

Like many of the rides at Theme Farm, this one was designed to be easily reconfigured, to keep up with topical issues. Your journey might take you in a totally different direction on any given day. You might go on a futile hunt for an honest politician one day, then explore the joys of living below the poverty line the next. On this particular morning, we would be traveling through time for an up-close look at an extinct species: *The American Housewife of the 1960s.*

At the entrance was a huge, bronze statue of a suburban housewife, of a half-century ago. Standing proudly in a kitchen apron, she held a frying pan tightly in a rubber-gloved fist, while balancing a screaming toddler on her hip. Her determined expression showed the resolve of a soldier ready to march into battle.

Back then, housewives were perceived as the very symbol of contentment. They seemed to have it all, but actually had very few freedoms. Before the decade was out, mothers, daughters, and wives would organize to form the Women's Liberation Movement, and protest by burning bras and marching on Washington for equal rights.

And I thought only teenagers rebelled!

Behind the statue was the point of departure for an excursion into the wilds of 1960s America. Theme park guests boarded a rugged landrover, like the ones you see in National Geographic on the plains of the Serengeti, but with seating for a dozen passengers.

I took a sip of my Jiffy Fizz Cola and got in line.

A group of brave adventurers were just return- ing from the perilous journey, and the jungle jeep was ready to take on another load of passengers. Behind the wheel was a petite, lady Fritter, whose slender shoulders supported the long neck of a giraffe.

"All aboard!" she said into a microphone. "The next jungle adventure departs in three minutes."

Her name was Miss Sally Bronson, but everyone called her *Long Tall Sally*. She had been my History teacher in school before taking on work as a Theme Farm ride operator.

After earning their American citizenship, Fritterz were tolerated by most humans, but a deep-rooted "fritterphobia" continued to linger just below the surface. Taking the teaching job was a risky move for Sally. Unfortunately, the endless harassment and rude pranks from students and teachers forced her to quit. Too bad. She was my favorite teacher.

"Room for one more?" I asked Sally.

"Amy!" she said excitedly. "I haven't seen you in ages. What brings you out to Theme Farm?"

"Answers," I said. "I want to learn all there is to know about the 1960s."

"Well, you've come to the right place, and this is the perfect ride to get you started. Get in."

I took a seat right behind Sally and buckled my seatbelt.

"You'll have to leave that behind," she said, pointing to the beverage in my hand.

I started to toss it into a trash bin, then looked at the blue can and decided to conduct a little test.

"Did you know that Jiffy Fizz cans used to be red?" I said to Sally, studying her reaction.

"Where have *you* been," she said, laughing. "They've *always* been blue."

With her jungle jeep now full of novice explorers, Sally picked up her mic and turned to her passengers. "Everybody ready? Here we go."

The vehicle's powerful engine raced as Sally slammed it into gear. The jeep lurched forward, and we were on our way.

The ride began by trudging down a bumpy, muddy road that cut through a dark jungle. My skin moistened from the thick, muggy air. The sounds of wild birds and the grunts of ferocious animals were heard all around us.

"Please keep your seatbelts fastened," Sally advised her passengers. "I may have to make sudden turns to avoid the rare species of frogs that inhabit the jungle floor. They are easily angered, and I'm not good at dealing with *Toad* Rage."

The group chuckled and groaned at the same time.

"The creatures we will be encountering today are either already extinct, or high on the endangered humans list," explained Sally. "You may be shocked at what you see. Many will be in awe. But all of you will be touched by their uncanny ability to survive in the wild. Most haven't been seen since the early '60s, so keep a watchful eye out."

The jeep slowed. We could just make out the sound of someone humming in a field of tall grass.

"Sh!" said Sally, her finger to her lips. "Get out your cameras. You are about to witness one of your distant relatives going about her daily routine."

A clearing came into view that revealed a young woman. The animatronic figure was standing at an ironing board, surrounded by clotheslines, sagging from the weight of scores of shirts, pants, and bed sheets. She cheerfully hummed as she ironed, as the workload ahead of her gently swayed in the breeze.

"What a break," whispered Sally. "This unusual behavior is rarely seen today. Notice how happy this specimen is. Being a domesticated breed, housewives gladly accepted the drudgery of house-work."

The jeep picked up speed, and we were soon on a flat plain that stretched for miles. On a grassy knoll, under a shade tree, a group of women sat in a circle on folding chairs. One dominant female stood in the center of them.

"Here's a typical example of social interaction within the species," said Sally. "Often referred to as *parties,* these gatherings were really nothing more than sales presentations." The lead woman snapped a lid onto a plastic bowl, while her giddy guests applauded with delight. "With the tight, grocery budgets imposed on housewives by their mates, preserving unfinished meals was a necessity. With this storage innovation, leftovers would stay fresh for days."

We next traveled over a desert landscape. Off to one side, in a deep trench, men in pith helmets were digging at the dry earth.

"Here," said Sally, "an anthropological dig is underway. This excavation has uncovered rare, mid-century kitchen artifacts. Notice the labor-saving devices, like easy-clean ovens, motorized vegetable slicers, and faucets that dispensed dish soap right out of the tap."

Sally further remarked that replicas of these items could be purchased in the gift shop at the end of the ride.

Just ahead was a single-family tract house, like the thousands that were built during that decade. We slowed down as Sally described the scene:

"It was once thought that '60s housewives hibernated, since they were rarely seen outside of their above-ground dens. We now know that she was doing anything but sleeping, as demonstrated by this family unit in their natural habitat."

The jeep crept past the living room window. Inside, a man rested comfortably in an easy chair. His slippered feet were propped up on a padded foot stool, as he puffed smoke rings from a tobacco pipe.

"Notice the dominance of the male," said Sally. "Having fathered several offspring, it was natural to assign the rearing of the children to the female."

Passing by another window, a boy and girl were lying on the floor watching *Beany and Cecil* cartoons on a black and white TV.

The kitchen then came into view, where a woman stood over a hot stove. Steam from boiling pots and pans filled the small space, as she wiped the sweat from her brow.

"It was once thought that females were happy

with this arrangement," said Sally, "but research has proven otherwise. They actually detested it. But change was in the wind, and women of the '60s would soon raise their voices in protest."

The jeep came to a halt as we encountered a rushing river in our path. The water didn't appear too deep that our sturdy vehicle couldn't easily cross it, so we ventured onward. But halfway across, the engine suddenly stalled.

"Uh oh!" said Sally. "This couldn't happen in a worse place."

I heard a faint, distant murmuring in the dense brush behind us. It got increasingly louder as Sally tried to get the engine going again.

Suddenly, an object flew over our heads. It was a golf club.

"Get down!," shouted Sally. "We're in Liberation Country."

The murmuring turned to angry chanting, like a primitive jungle tribe on the hunt. More projectiles came at us: tennis rackets, poker chips, racetrack programs.

Sally tried repeatedly to get the jeep started, but the engine wouldn't turn over. Flaming bras and girdles flew overhead like Molotov cocktails. The message of the chanting became clearer:

"Rights for women!"

"Rights for women!"

Finally, the engine started. Sally grinded the

gears. "Hang on!"

A moment later, we were safely on the outer bank. The threatening voices stopped. We all let out a collective sigh of relief, just as a bowling ball landed in the river next to us, creating a wave of water that soaked everyone in the jeep.

My fellow passengers and I arrived back at Base Camp—laughing, while showing off our damp clothes to each other.

As I unbuckled my seatbelt, Sally placed her hand on my shoulder. "Wait here, Amy," she said. Then she announced to the others: "Thank you for joining me today. For those of you who got wet, I would offer you a towel, but I have a *dry* sense of humor."

Half-laughing and half-moaning, the passengers disembarked.

I stayed in the jeep as Sally pulled up to the next group of passengers, but she wouldn't allow them to board.

"Sorry folks," she said to the waiting crowd, "We are currently experiencing technical difficulties, and the ride will be down for some time. Please try back later."

Then Sally and I drove off alone.

We passed through a tall gate into the ride's backstage area, where I got a rare glimpse at the behind-the-scenes operations. I saw the long hoses from air compressors that gave life to the robotic characters. Dozens of sound effect speakers were hidden among the jungle foliage. The best part was seeing the huge air cannons that launched women's undergarments at stranded travelers.

Sally looked over at me. "There's something wrong, isn't there, Amy?" she said.

"How did you guess?"

"I noticed you twisting your hair with your finger during the ride. You used to do the same thing in class when something was bothering you."

Sally turned a corner, and we were behind the tract house. The rigid animatronic figures, looking eerily human, were turned off.

"Here's your stop," said Sally.

"What do you mean?"

"End of the line. Everybody out."

I looked at her, baffled, but stepped off the jeep like she asked.

"Now what?" I said.

"Only Theme Farm would know," she answered, then drove away.

I stood there alone in the spooky quietness. There were no jungle sound effects, and no rushing water noise from the stream, that was now a dry riverbed.

Then I heard a voice. "Kinda creepy out here, isn't it?"

It seemed to come in the direction of the mechanical housewife, but she wasn't moving.

Then I heard the voice again. "I'm talking to you, Amy!"

Someone was standing behind me.

I jumped as I spun around. "Man!" I said, "Don't sneak up on people like that." I was speaking to a woman, who looked awfully familiar.

"Don't you recognize me, Amy?" said the intruder from out of nowhere.

Suddenly, I realized that I *did* know her. She was my grandmother, as a young woman! I recognized her from an old photo I had of her when she was in her 20s. She worked as a model back then. The picture was clipped from a Ford dealership catalog. It showed her happily waving while riding in the back seat of a Lincoln Continental convertible.

"Grandma?" I said. "Is that you?"

She smiled. "How did you like the ride?"

"Never mind that!" I said. "How can you be here?"

"You mean, because I'm dead? If I remember correctly, you were about 3 years old when I kicked the bucket."

"Then you *can't* be who you say you are. You're a robot, like these other fake human figures around here."

"So sure of everything, aren't you? Just like your mother."

I reached out to poke her face with my finger to see if it was made of rubber, but she held up her hand and stopped me.

"See that character over there?" she said, pointing to the frazzled woman in the kitchen. "That was me in the early '60s, just after I married your grandfather. I was barely 18 when I took the plunge."

"You were married that young?" I said.

"I didn't want to, but single women living alone was considered daring in those days, and I wanted my independence more that anything in the world—just like you do."

"How do you know about *that*?"

"Grandmothers know everything. I know about Clifford, Hubert, Sally, even Zeb the Abra-ca-zebra. But mostly, I know what's in your heart."

I was too young to have known Grandma before she died, and I had no memory of her. Whoever, or whatever I was talking to was no more real than those human-looking machines around me. But real or fake, I was moved by her presence, nonetheless.

"How's your mother?" asked Grandma.

"She hates me!" I said. "That's why I want to move out. She would sooner see me dead than spend one more day with me in that house."

"Oh, that can't be true. I brought her up better than that."

"Okay, maybe I'm exaggerating. Let's just say there's no love lost between us. I don't connect with her anymore."

"That's not possible. There's an inseparable bond that exists between all mothers and daughters. Deny it all you want, but it's there, and will be for as long as you live. You're problem is that you only see her as a mother, instead of a human being with feelings. And by the way, she *doesn't* want you to move out. No mother, no matter the circumstances, wants to see her young leave the nest."

"But I *want* to leave the nest."

"I know it gets pretty cramped in there as we get older. There never seems to be room enough to do all that we want. But the key is to *make* room. You'd be surprised how roomy the nest can be when you share it. Patience, Amy. The time will come for you to be on your own, but not now."

"But *you* did it in the '60s."

"Good lord, child! The '60s went extinct long ago. You're living in the past. Try living in the here-and-now for a change."

Real or not, this was one grandmother who told it like it is—and it was definitely what I needed to hear. I was grateful for that.

I stepped forward and put my arms around her, but they passed right through her body. Then she started to fade away like a vanishing wisp of smoke in the wind.

"You forgot, didn't you?" said Grandma.

"Forgot what?"

She was almost invisible now, as her voice trailed off.

"Embrace today, for you cannot touch the past."

Chapter 9

Like Music

*T*een fashion in the early '60s was totally bizarre. I searched through photos from old teen magazines from that part of the decade. What I found was a lot of teenage girls in plain cotton blouses and plaid skirts. It seemed like the youth of that time hadn't yet found their own fashion identity. Regardless, I thought it might be fun to dress like the girls of Clifford's time, if I was going to keep seeing him.

Miniskirts and Go-go Boots were not yet in vogue. "Mod" fashions wouldn't take off until '64. So, I decided to stay with a more conservative look. I found a sleeveless scoop neck dress in a retro clothing boutique that was just perfect. As long as I was dressing the part, I thought I would do a little '60s-style primping, too. I put on mascara and blue eye shadow. I even went so far as to hot-curl a bouffant flip at the ends of my hair. Actually, it looked kinda cute. I was starting to like the '60s!

I was surprised to see other people dressed in '60s garb, in line for Used-to-Be TV—and not just kids. An older gentleman ahead of me donned a tailored, gabardine suit, with a hat Frank Sinatra might have worn. Maybe he had arranged a rendezvous with a rich widow in 1963. His heavy cologne definitely suggested a romantic encounter of some kind. I guess no one told him that smells don't travel over television.

The lines were getting longer every day as the attraction gained popularity. I was late for my noontime appointment with Clifford, so I shoved past the others in line. I bypassed the pre-show presentation, pushed through a side door, finally arriving at my usual cottage. I turned the door knob to go inside, but it wouldn't budge. The door was locked! I looked through the window, and immediately felt my blood pressure rise. Imagine my outrage to see another girl on the couch talking to Clifford!

A streak of jealousy roared up my spine, but there was no good reason for it. For one thing, they couldn't be saying anything of any significance without the magic clicker. For another, why *shouldn't* Clifford talk to someone else? I had no exclusive claim on him. If he found someone he liked better than me, well, it's his life. I was proud of myself for taking such a grownup attitude toward the whole thing.

Still . . .

If that little bitch didn't unlock the door in exactly one minute, I was going to break it down!

Fortunately, that wouldn't be necessary. I watched as that little home wrecker got up off the couch and walked to the door. I played the innocent bystander as she passed me.

"Who was that?" I asked, showing interest in Clifford. "He's sort of awesome-looking, don't ya think?"

"Don't waste your time, girl," she said. "He's a dweeb."

Good! That was just what I wanted to hear.

I went inside, locked the door behind me, and raced over to the couch.

Ping! went the clicker.

Clifford wasn't in his chair. I feared he had gotten tired of waiting for me, and gone home, but I waited dutifully in front of the TV until I knew for sure.

I crossed my legs, put one arm over the back of the couch, and flung my head back like a high-fashion model. My silky, flipped-up hair flowed down my back like a sexy woman in a hair care commercial. Wait till he gets a load of me, I thought. Now he'll see how much classier I am over that other girl.

Five minutes passed, and still no Clifford. It was

time to start worrying.

I stood up and paced the floor. Then I heard music coming from the TV speaker. The sound was tinny and scratchy. A piano was playing a catchy, little tune that I did not recognize.

Then Clifford leaned into frame, holding a portable tape recorder. It was the old-fashioned type with the spinning, half-dollar-sized reels—like the ones on the old *Mission Impossible* TV series.

I composed myself and sat down. "Is that you, playing?" I asked.

"Yeah," said Clifford, taking his seat. "I wrote it last night. It doesn't sound too good, I know."

"Sounds okay to me. It's not digital, but what can you do?"

"Digital?"

"Ah . . . delightful, I meant to say. Your playing is delightful!"

The song ended, and Clifford shut off his machine.

We stared at each other in silence for a moment.

"How long have you been out there?" asked Clifford nervously.

"Why do you ask?" I said, knowing full well where his questioning was headed.

"Oh, just wondering."

"Just wondering if I caught you with that other girl?" I asked, a little pissed off.

Clifford gulped. "You saw?"

"Yes, I saw! What were you two talking about?"

"Nothing. Why are you so upset? I didn't do anything wrong."

"I'm not upset!" I shouted. "I'm just—"

"You're mad because you thought I might prefer someone else over you. Isn't that it? Why don't you just tell me the truth?"

I had always prided myself on being straightforward and honest, yet there I was, hiding behind some silly, adolescent pride. I was as jealous as I could be, and I should have told him so from the start.

"I'm sorry, Cliff," I said. "I shouldn't be intruding on your life like this. It's just that when you find yourself attracted to someone, you're not so quick to give him up."

"I'm sorry, too, Amy," said Clifford. "I shouldn't have beat around the bush about having spoken to that girl. I was afraid that if you knew, you'd never speak to me again, and I couldn't live with that."

I felt like a schoolgirl on her first date, speaking candidly with a boy for the first time. We were finally confessing our true feelings for each other.

It was my turn to say something, but I was too flustered to speak.

Clifford finally broke the ice. "You look nice today, Amy," he said.

"You, too," I said.

Clifford was wearing a tweed sports jacket over a

turtleneck sweater, with pleated dress slacks—like he had stripped a mannequin naked in the men's department at Macy's. His hair was neatly combed, though still showing a trace of that greasy hair goo. Obviously, he was trying to make as good of an impression on me, as I was on him.

But it didn't feel right. There was something phony about our appearance.

"This is ridiculous," I said. "I shouldn't have put on this outfit for you. It's not me. Not me at all!"

"I'm guilty of the same thing," said Clifford. "I overdressed to make you think I'm someone I'm not."

Another moment of silence.

Clifford stared at the ground, deep in thought. "There's lyrics to that song, you know."

"There is?" I said. "How do they go? Did you record it? What's the song called?"

"It's called '*Your Love, Like Music.*'" Then Clifford drew an incredibly long breath. "I wrote it . . . for *you!*"

I almost fell off the couch! A song? For me?

"You want to hear it?" asked Clifford.

"More than anything!"

I got chills of anticipation as he fast-forwarded the tape.

He hit the Play button, and after a lively piano introduction, Clifford's voice on the tape sang this lovely melody:

I hear your voice
Singing in my ear
Never will I hear
A sweeter sound.

I hear a song
When you call my name
Since the day you came
Around.

Your love, like music
Like sweet melodies
Dancing on the keys
Of my piano.

Your love, like music
Let the music play
Forever you will stay
In my heart.

I felt like Juliet being serenaded by Romeo. The song was simple and sweet, and the romantic lyrics went straight to my heart.

Clifford hit the Stop button. "That's enough."

"No, please!" I begged him. "Play the rest of it."

Clifford's shyness had been like a dark cloud that followed him everywhere, always blocking the sunlight on a perfect day. But all that was about to change. He sat up tall, with a self-confidence I hadn't seen in him till now. He smiled at me and nodded, and the transformation was complete. The timid boy with the yo-yo was gone forever.

I heard the click of the Play button.

I see your face
And suddenly I hear
A big band loud and clear
in the park.

I feel the beat
Won't you come with me
Dancing in the street
After dark.

Your love, like music
Like sweet melodies
Dancing on the keys
Of my piano.

Your love, like music,
Let the music play
Forever you will stay
Forever you will stay
Forever . . . in my heart.

Clifford snapped off the recorder. He was clearly as moved as I was.

I instinctively reached my hand out to him. Then

I was suddenly overwhelmed by a terrible feeling: That devastating moment the magic zebra had warned me about had arrived. There would be no embracing, no touching of any kind. Clifford had given me a beautiful gift few will ever receive, and I couldn't even shake his hand to thank him. I so desperately wanted to caress his cheek. I would even have overlooked the grease in his hair to run my fingers through it.

Clifford, too, was hopelessly trying to reach out to me beyond time and space.

I pulled my hand back and covered my mouth to hide my sorrow. "What are we gonna do?"

"I wish I knew, Amy," sighed Clifford.

"I feel so close to you right now, yet so far away at the same time. It's a long way to Dorian."

"Not really. The physical space between us isn't far at all. It's kinda funny, actually. You're fifty years in the future, and yet it's like you're sitting right here next to me."

"I don't want to talk any more about it. It's too painful."

Clifford smiled gently. "Don't be sad, Amy. When you get home tonight, go outside and look up at the moon. It hasn't changed in a million years. I'll be looking at that same moon, and my face will look down on yours. I'll be winking at you through the twinkling stars. The heavens are timeless, and it is there we will find togetherness."

Clifford certainly had a way with words. His inspired speech had soothed my grief-stricken heart. He may have been a dweeb, like that brash young woman said, but he had the healing powers of a poet.

"Same time tomorrow?" I said.

"I'll be waiting."

Chapter 10

Mom

The night was calm, and everyone in the house was asleep. No noise. No distractions. The perfect conditions for reading. My book of choice for that evening was titled *1963: The Year in Perspective*. If I was going to know Clifford's world better, I needed to get familiar with the times he was living in.

I already knew most of the historical events that took place, like the Vietnam War and the Civil Rights March on Washington. But it was the less significant things—the styles, the trends, the culture—that I most wanted to learn about.

Surfing was becoming a favorite teen pastime. The Beach Boys were "Surfin' USA" on *FM* car radios—a new innovation introduced that year. Families gathered around their TVs for an evening of *Bonanza*, *The Dick Van Dyke Show*, and *Walt Disney's Wonderful World of Color*. For more exhilarating entertainment, Alfred Hitchcock's *The Birds* had audiences cowering behind their seats at the local cinema. Radio stations had just started playing records by a little-known, British rock band called *The Beatles*.

It was a happy and prosperous time to be alive. Smiley faces were everywhere. But the dark times ahead were foreshadowed when the year closed with the assassination of President Kennedy.

The book slip through my fingers as I started to nod off. After a long, sustained yawn, I bookmarked my place with the old photo of my 20-something grandmother, smiling in the back seat of a luxury car.

I must have been smiling in my sleep. I dreamed that I was watching the Ed Sullivan TV show in 1963. The night's lineup included Jim Henson's Muppets, comedy duo Allen & Rossi, Topo Gigio the Italian mouse, and singing sensation *Clifford Anderson*.

"And now," said Mr. Sullivan, "right here on our stage, all the way from Dorian, here are Clifford Anderson and the Cliffettes!"

The teenage studio audience screamed their lungs out. Clifford was played onto the stage by a 50-piece orchestra. Before he began his first number, he signaled the band to stop, waved the audience into silence, then looked straight into the camera and said, "This song's for you, Amy."

I was awakened from my fantasy slumber when I heard a bump in the hallway. I threw back my covers, crept to the door, and opened it slowly. There was my mom, in pink pajama pants and a Led Zeppelin t-shirt, reaching behind a flower pot on the floor.

"Mom," I said. "What are you doing out here at this hour?"

"I couldn't sleep," she said, straightening up. "I was going downstairs for a snack, when this caught the corner of my eye." She held up a ring—not a valuable one, but a cheap knickknack. "I've been looking for this for years."

"What is it?" I asked.

Mom held it close to her heart and glowed. "Your father gave it to me when we first met."

"That?" I said, pointing to the worthless jewelry. "He must have been a cheap date."

"Neither of us could afford much back then. We kept this ring a secret between us. I was too embarrassed to show it to anyone."

"Wise decision. That thing's worth a dime if even that."

My mom gave me a crabby look. "What do *you* know about it," she said. "When you're in love, it's the sentiment that matters. I don't suppose you know anything about that."

"What makes you think I don't?"

Mom leaned into my face. "You've got that look

in your eye," she said. "There's a boy, isn't there?" I looked away. "Why didn't you tell me?"

"You never asked," I said.

My mother looked down at the sentimental keepsake in her hand, then grinned. "Join me in a cup of hot chocolate?" she asked. But before I could answer, she grabbed my hand and led me downstairs to the kitchen.

I sat on a kitchen bar stool in my purple night-shirt, while Mom popped two slices of bread into the toaster. Then she made our hot chocolate—not from a cheap, tear-open package, but with real, dark chocolate from a tin.

This was a mother-daughter nighttime ritual we had shared since I was a little girl. But in the midst of our current legal battle it felt awkward. I hadn't spoken at length with my mom in months. Now, we were about to have an intimate conversation, and I was a little uneasy about it.

Mom brought our steaming, chocolate treats to the counter, plopped a marshmallow into each cup, then sat down on the stool next to me. I spread apple butter and cinnamon on our toast, just like I had always done. Dad's sorrowful-looking ring lay on the counter between us.

Then mom opened a drawer and pulled out a large photo album, that I had seen a hundred times before.

"I'll prove my story to you about the ring," said

Mom, opening the album.

The photos were kept in place with white, corner stickers. The first in the collection were old Polaroid snapshots.

"Look there, on my finger," said Mom. The faded image showed my youthful mother holding out her hand, and sure enough, there was the plastic ring.

"So *that's* what this picture is all about," I said.

"Your dad was a young writer," said Mom, "and I was a secretary at a small publishing house. He had submitted a manuscript for his new book, and had come to see if anyone had read it. The editor said he had, and in a very nice way, told him that it sucked. But I read it and loved it, and I told him so."

"Let me guess," I said. "He was so moved by your praise that he asked you to dinner. But he barely had a dollar to spend, but you didn't care. Just being with him was like walking on air. And as a token of his affection, he got you this ring out of a bubble gum dispenser. And as he placed it on your finger, it was like you had been given the Crown Jewels. How close am I?"

"Pretty close, except you left out one detail."

"What's that?"

"We *did* have a splendid dinner that night, and at one of the finest restaurants in town."

"I thought you said Dad was broke."

"I paid."

We shared a quick laugh together, something we hadn't done in a long time. Then it got quiet, remembering that we were supposed to be bitter rivals. We had exchanged a few, nice words, but we had also said other things in recent months that *weren't* so nice—in and out of courtrooms.

"We probably shouldn't be talking like this," said Mom, "but I've been fortunate to have true love in my life, and I want you to know that it's something I pray you'll find someday, too."

I hesitated before volunteering any information about Clifford. But I figured, what have I got to lose?

"What if I told you I already have?" I said.

Mom gave me a surprised look. "Really? Who is he?"

The circumstances were too incredible for me to go into detail. Still, mothers and daughters are suppose to confide in each other in matters of the heart.

"Well," I said, "it's a little complicated, but—"

Mom put up her hand. "Say no more," she said. "It's a personal matter and I shouldn't pry."

But I *wanted* her to pry. I wanted to give her a chance to shed tears of joy for me, or lecture me for being too immature, or scold me for making the biggest mistake of my life. I longed to experience that closeness you're suppose to feel with your mom. But how could I tell her about Cliff?

Just then, Mom splashed a spot of hot chocolate on her nightwear.

"Oh, look what I did," she said. "I'll be right back. I'm just gonna go rinse this out." Then she disappeared into the laundry room.

While I waited for her return, I thumbed through the old album. Her whole courtship with Dad was chronicled in pictures. Jammed between the pages were personal mementos: movie ticket stubs, pressed flowers, restaurant napkins.

The wedding photos came next: the bridal party posing with the bride and groom; Mom throwing her flower bouquet; Dad tossing my mom's garter in the same manner.

Then came the children's photo history. My siblings and I each had our own pages in the album. The photos in each section weren't much different from the others, highlighting typical childhood milestones: your first pony ride, your first day at summer camp, and your first time riding a bike without falling over.

I then came to the section with *Amy* across the top of the first page, but something was horribly wrong. The page was empty! The white, corner stickers were there, but the photos were gone. The pages that followed were also empty. I had been erased from the family album!

I skipped to the back where my birth certificate had been mounted. It was gone, too! My brother and sister's certificates hadn't been touched.

My falling out with my parents was more hurtful to my mom than I realized—and here was the proof. Our relationship had been hanging by a thread as it was, then I had to come along and sever it.

Maybe it was time we started communicating.

I closed the album, just as my mom returned to the kitchen. We had spent such a pleasant time together, I didn't want to spoil it by bringing up what I had just seen.

My mom reached for the album to put it away, when I placed my hand over hers.

"Mom?" I said. "What's happen to us?"

Her lower lip quivered. Then she threw her arms around me, and gave me the biggest hug I can remember ever getting from her.

Tears filled my eyes as I hugged her back. "I thought that leaving home was what I wanted," I said. "Now I'm not so sure."

Mom looked at me, then cradled my face in her hands. "It's okay, Amy," she said. "How things got to this point, I'm not sure. I suppose I'm to blame as much as anyone. But your dad and I taught you to follow your own path, and where you go from here is up to you. Don't worry too much about me. You have love in your life, and that makes me happy. And if someday you should ever have children of your own . . ."

Mom's voice went suddenly silent. Her expression darkened, like a sinister shadow had passed over her face.

"What is it, Mom?" I said, frightened.

She grabbed the handle of her cup. "Nothing," she said coldly.

"Was it something I said?"

"No."

She got up without uttering another word, tossed her cinnamon toast in the trash, and poured the rest of her chocolate down the sink. Then she walked out of the kitchen.

I picked the ring up off the counter as she started for the stairs. Grabbing hold of her arm, I held up the cherished reminder of her past.

"You forgot this," I said.

She looked over her shoulder at me, slowly lifted the ring out of my hand, then placed in on her little finger. Her eyes shimmered as she stared at it wistfully.

"We all have our secrets, Amy," was all Mom would say. Then she continued up the stairs.

I went back to the kitchen to clean up what was left of a bewildering evening. I put the photo album back in its drawer. Whatever dark secret Mom was hiding, those photos held no clue.

Chapter 11

Telling Hubert

I hadn't told a living soul about the magic clicker. The only other people who knew it existed was Bob Phillips and Zeb, the half-zebra—if indeed he existed at all. But the deeper I got involved with Clifford, the more I felt the need to confide in someone with what I was up to. Hubert was the only person I could trust to keep my secret.

Hubert and I had just gotten off the *Spit Buckets* —a Theme Farm ride where an overhead skyway transports guests across the park. The buckets were actually oversized, cow-milking pails suspended from cables high above the ground.

While skyways are a common sight at theme parks, they usually prove to be a major headache for Management. Countless complaints are routinely filed by park guests who have been spat upon by discourteous riders. Theme Farm took a different approach to this problem. The park regarded this tasteless behavior as a form of free expression, and since people were going to do it anyway, why not encourage it? The difference was that the Spit Bucket ride employed an invisible shield that prevented the wet projectiles from ever reaching the ground, keeping the unsuspecting guests below comfortably dry.

We had just exited the ride as our stomachs were telling us: "Lunch, please!"

"Suppose we try *Democracy Diner* today," I said.

This was one of our favorite Theme Farm restaurants. It's the only place I know where you are served a tasty meal while getting a lesson in Civics at the same time. Liberals are seated on the left; Conservatives to the right; counter seating is reserved for Independents only. Menu specials include the *Presidential Veto Burrito* and *Rhetoric on a Stick.* I "elected" to order the *Minority Whip Dip,* while Hubert got the *Sex Scandal Platter.* For dessert, we voted unanimously to each get a slice of the diner's most popular dessert: *Impeachment Pie.*

This was as good a time as any to let Hubert in on my covert activity.

"Remember that Theme Farm attraction you told me about," I asked him, "Used-to-Be TV?"

"I hear that communicating with anyone on it is pretty fruitless," said Hubert. "There's some kind of detection system that censors anything it doesn't want you to say. A constant bleeping keeps a slip of the lip from changing history."

"That's true. But what if I told you I didn't have that problem?"

"I'd say that would be very dangerous. Can you really say whatever you want to people in the past?"

"Yes, I can. And it *is* dangerous. You may not believe this, but I said something stupid that changed the color of Jiffy Fizz Cola cans from red to blue."

Hubert smiled and shook his head. "What do mean, red? The color of their cans is a universal trademark. They've *always* been blue . . . haven't they?"

Hubert wasn't smiling now.

I pulled the magic clicker out of my pocket.

"What's that?" asked Hubert.

"The device that can change history."

"Can I see it?"

"If you're careful."

I checked to see if anyone was watching us before I handed the clicker to Hubert. He put it up to his eye, checking it out from end to end.

"I don't suppose you'll let me see inside," said the incurable tinkerer.

"Better not," I said. "I don't know how fragile it is, and as far as I know it's the only one there is."

"How do you work it?"

"You aim it at any TV in the attraction, hit that button, and you can speak freely with whomever is on the screen with no bleeping. I've been using it to talk to a boy I met in 1963."

Hubert looked at me with deadly seriousness. "How much have you told him about the future?"

"Not much."

"Not much could turn into a whole lot if you're not careful. That was a pivotal time in American history. I hope you're not thinking of meddling with the '60s."

"There is a certain power you feel with this clicker in your hand. I don't deny it. But I've resisted the urge to give away any damaging information. The Jiffy Fizz thing was just kind of an accident."

"You idiot!" snarled Hubert. "I should destroy this thing right now."

"Don't you dare!" I yelled, grabbing the device out of his hand.

"An accident, you say!" said Hubert, his face red with rage. "You burn yourself on a stove. That's an accident. You hit the wrong number while dialing a phone. That's an accident, too. We can recover from those. The Fukushima nuclear power plant melt down. Even *that* we can survive. But you reveal one slip up about the future, in some stupid theme park ride, and your 'accident' will be permanent."

Hubert had put into words what I did not want to admit to myself. I was playing with fire, like a willful child who should know better. Changing the color of a soda can was one thing, but changing the landscape of the future was quite another.

"But I *can't* destroy the clicker," I said.

"Why not?"

"Because I will also be destroying the sunshine of my life."

"Oh, no!" said Hubert, his hand on his forehead. "Don't tell me. You've fallen for some schlep in 1963."

I bowed my head while raising my eyes up at Hubert, like a puppy that just got caught soiling the carpet.

"I should have known," he said. "You always make the worst choices when it comes to boys. When are you going to start listening to your head instead of your heart?"

Under normal circumstances, I would have stood up to Hubert and defended my integrity. I would have blasted him with a million reasons why he was wrong—only this time he wasn't. I was in way over my head, and I knew it.

"You don't have to be so cruel," I said.

Hubert placed his hand on my shoulder. "I'm sorry, Amy," he said softly. "You're the last person I would ever want to hurt. I just want you to understand how serious this is."

"You haven't told me anything I don't already know. I just wish I knew what to do about it."

"Tell you what. I don't agree with what you are doing, but if you ever get the urge to alter history, I want you to call me. I'll be your own personal support group. It'll be like Alcoholics Anonymous for people who want to destroy life as we know it. Okay?"

"Okay, Hubert. I'll call you if I start to get the shakes."

"Promise?"

"I promise."

Chapter 12

Time Lapse

November.
The corn had been harvested and the sheep had been sheared. The cows were in the meadow and the hay was in the barn—and I was back at Shanksonville High School.

What direction my personal life would take was still up in the air. After much haggling with Judge Higgins, Bob Phillips had finally gotten me a court date on the Family Court calendar. My final emancipation hearing would take place at the end of the month.

At home, I held my breath every time I walked through the front door. My parents and I had simply stopped talking to each other. All there was to say had already been said.

Now it was just a waiting game to see how the judge would rule.

It was also November in Dorian. Between

school activities and homework, Clifford and I decided to limit our get-togethers to weekends. He was in his final year of high school, and looking ahead to college. Furthering his music education was a natural choice. He had already won a few professional writing contracts, composing jingles for radio commercials.

1963 saw the birth of a revolution in music. Bob Dylan, Peter, Paul, and Mary, and other musical talents were gaining in popularity with their politically-charged protest songs. Now politically active himself, Clifford joined this dissident movement. It was totally unlike him, but I didn't complain. I had watched this introverted boy blossom into a concerned young adult, and it was good to see him climb out of his shell.

I was also impressed by how much Clifford's songwriting chops had improved. I was a little bias, of course, being his inspiration for much of his best work. There was no shortage of joyful, up-tempo tunes:

"You Make Me Smile"

> *I looked up to the sky*
> *The sun was shining through*
> *And we will be alright*
> *'Cause now I see the light in you.*

"By The Time You Get This Letter"

If you feel the way I do
Then I'll be yours forevermore
I'll be at your side
To keep you satisfied
Until I'm ninety-four.

"As Long As You Come Back To Me"

You say you wanna get out for a while
You wanna set your spirit free
Well don't you know it's alright
As long as you come back to me.

As always, I was mindful not to tell Clifford too much about the future. Occasionally, however, comments would leak out regarding the social and political turmoil of my time. They didn't seem to cause any major upheavals in the world that I could see, although they definitely influenced Clifford's writing:

"What I'll Do For You"

While Congress relaxes
After raising your taxes
I'll veto it for you.

And you feel like a chump
As you pay at the pump
I'll fix all that, too.

But the change in seasons also brought a change in Clifford's attitude toward life. The rise of the '60s counterculture was just picking up steam. Rebellious young people were searching for their own identities. Clifford, too, was struggling to find his voice through his music. Fewer of his songs spoke of love and happiness, and more commented on his turbulent times.

He attacked the Establishment:

"The Jail Song"

Post your bail
Or rot away in jail
How'd I get myself in this jam.

What the hell
I'm sitting in this cell
No one gives a damn.

The Vietnam War was also a target:

"Compassion"

I've seen the rain
The darkness and the light
I've felt the pain of being alone.

I've heard the cries
Of children in the night
Follow me
Follow me.

The cottage TV faded up on 1963. There was Clifford, slouching in his chair, his eyes hidden behind dark sunglasses. On the back wall of his office hung a large Peace Sign, along with protest posters and bumper stickers that read *We Shall Overcome!* and *Make Love Not War!*

Clifford's appearance had changed radically. His hair was long and shaggy, with bushy sideburns that ran all the way down to his chin.

"How ya doing, Cliff," I said.

"What's shakin', baby," said Clifford, in his beatnik-style voice.

"A funny thing happen at school last week. I had a long talk with my old friend, Lydia, that involved you. You want to hear about it?"

"Sure . . . I guess," said Clifford, disinterested.

"Lydia isn't my closest friend, but we usually share what's going on in our love lives. Well, I hadn't shared anything with her lately, and she was growing suspicious—"

Clifford kept looking away as I was talking. He fidgeted in his chair, like a toddler in need of an afternoon nap.

"Are you listening to me?" I asked.

"Yeah, yeah," he said.

"What's the matter?"

"Nothin'."

"Something's wrong. Why don't you get it off your chest?"

Clifford sat up in his chair. I gave him my full attention.

"Alright," he said. "Here it is: I turned 18 yesterday."

"You did?" I said, delighted. "Congratulations! Did you have a party?

"Hell, no! The guest of honor was in no mood for a party."

"Why not? Didn't get any presents?

"Indeed I did, including this." He held up an official government letter. It was from the Selective Service System: a federal government agency that requires all 18-year-olds to register for military duty. In the event of war, the military can call you into service at a moment's notice.

"I'm not even old enough to vote, for chrissake!" complained Clifford.

"What's the big deal?" I said. "Kids your age have to do the same thing here, too."

"It may be a minor inconvenience in your time, but it's a *very* big deal in mine. They say that the Vietnam War will get worse before it gets better. The army sends more soldiers over there every week. Drafting deadbeat protesters like me will be next.

His prediction was right, of course. Vietnam was probably the most unpopular war in our history. "Draft dodgers" would number in the thousands.

"I don't want to die in some war I don't believe in," said Clifford. "I could refuse to go when I'm called up, but they'll send me to prison if I do. I could move to Canada, but who wants to do that?"

"I wish there was something I could do to help," I said.

"There is!" Clifford leaned in close to the screen. "Nobody knows when the war's gonna end, but *you* do. If I knew that, I could find a way to postpone my induction until it's over."

"You know I can't tell you that. I've told you a lot about the future already."

"You haven't told me squat! You've told me about games you play on TV sets, and hand-held music boxes that will replace transistor radios. So what?"

"I'm afraid to tell you any more than that."

"You're such a square! You say you want to help me, then you say you won't. A few simple words from you could help a lot of people. Think of all the other lives you could save. Tell me, Amy, how does the Vietnam War end? Will we have a nuclear war with Russia? Will China get The Bomb?"

It was tempting. I *did* know how those things

would turn out, and between Clifford and I we might save some people. But his arrogance was a real turn-off. He had become way too radical to be trusted with what I knew. Still, the answers he wanted would be so easy for me to give him.

This might have been a good time to call Hubert.

"What if I told you everything you're asking for, and it backfires?" I said. "I could be screwing up my own world and not even know it."

"But you *will* know," said Clifford. "Give me the information I want. Then you can tell me if anything has changed when you come back tomorrow. Dig?"

But I didn't have to wait for tomorrow. I could search Hubert's tablet right now and know instantly what impact I was having on history. And the tablet was right there in my bag!

"I don't think that's such a good idea," I said, while slowly reaching into my bag, that was just out of Clifford's view. I grabbed hold of the tablet.

"Man-o-man," said Clifford. "And I thought you were so hip. You talk big about changing the world, but when it comes to doing something about it, you cop out."

I quietly placed the tablet on the coffee table and turned it on.

"That's not true," I said.

The home page popped up on the screen, with a

search engine window begging me for a keyword. I could reveal Clifford's whole future to him by typing in his name. I could search his song titles and tell him if he had found any success with them. Searching for the Vietnam War would show me everything Clifford wanted to know about it. But what else would it show? Would I find Clifford's name on a prison inmate roll? Would I find that he had turned tail toward Canada? Or even worse, would I find his name as one of the honored dead on the Vietnam Memorial?

My hands trembled as I reached for the touchscreen. I typed in the keyword *Vietnam,* but I was afraid to go on. I couldn't do it! I turned off the device and stuffed it back in my bag.

I felt a sense of relief for now, but what about later? That temptation to discover what awaits Clifford would always haunt me. The truth about one's future is something no one should know. If I were to learn Clifford's fate, I would feel obligated to tell him about it, and I didn't want that responsibility.

"You're not listening to me," said Clifford.

"I'm afraid I can't help you," I said.

"That figures. But that's okay. You just go on living in your computerized, self-indulgent world. Just don't expect me to be here the next time you flip on the TV."

I can't recall ever feeling rage and sadness at the

same time. My temper flared while my tears flowed. Our relationship had reached a crossroad, and neither of us was willing to let the other one pass. I was afraid that the most wonderful time in my life was coming to an end.

I couldn't look at Clifford any more. I reached for the TV's on-off knob.

"You're brushing me off. Is that what you're doing?" said Clifford.

I pulled my hand back. "And why shouldn't I?"

I reached for the knob again.

"No, wait!" cried Clifford. "I'm sorry, Amy. Forgive me. Okay, so I'm a little testy. You'd be the same way if you were in my shoes."

"Please, Cliff. Can't we forget about saving the world and go back to being friends?"

"Friends? I don't even know what that word means anymore. Voice your opinion now days and people don't want to be seen with you. My parents are the worst. They won't go to social events for fear of what people might say about me behind their backs. I feel like telling them: *I quit! I resign from this family!*"

I had heard that line before. I said those same words in a courtroom, not so long ago. The TV screen was no longer just an electronic tube. It was a mirror, with myself in the reflection.

"Same time tomorrow?" said Clifford.

"I'd like that."

Chapter 13

Two Amys

The County Clerk's office was right next to the courthouse. I went inside and entered a huge, open area, with a long counter that seemed to stretch for a mile. Behind it were rows of back-to-back office desks. The back wall supported floor-to-ceiling shelves jammed with 3-ring binders, all neatly alphabetized. Signs hung above the counter every fifteen feet or so, to guide confused customers like me where to go. I followed the signs, *Marriage Licenses, Real Estate Records, Divorce Records,* finally arriving at the one I was looking for: *Birth Certificates.*

Seated at a desk was an elderly, stone-faced woman, with her hair done up in a tight bun. Around her neck was a thin, pearl necklace attached to her reading glasses. She looked like one of those strict librarians, always shushing anyone speaking above a whisper.

All of the other desks were empty. It was the lunch hour.

"Excuse me, ma'am," I said to the bookish, old woman.

She was going over a document, making checks in the margins with a red pencil, like grading a test paper.

"Please, wait your turn!" she insisted—an odd thing to say, considering that no one else was in the room.

Finally, she stood up and waddled over to me. "What is it, young lady?"

"I'd like to know how to get a copy of a birth certificate?"

"Is it yours?"

"Yes."

"Duplicate copies are $25 dollars."

I handed her a twenty and a five. She printed out a receipt, whomped it with a rubber stamp, then handed it to me, along with a request form.

"Fill this out and return it to me," she said, then waddled back to her desk.

The form asked for general information: name, birth date, mother's maiden name, that kind of thing. I signed the bottom.

"Here you go!" I said, holding the form in the air.

"Please, wait your turn!" said the woman once again.

Returning to the counter, she snatched the form from my hand, then quickly scanned it with her cold, gray eyes.

"Do you have some identification, miss?" she asked.

I handed her my student ID card. She entered the contents of the form into a computer on the counter, then gracefully hit the enter key, like Liberace hitting the final note of a Beethoven concerto.

"Done," she said. "You'll have your certificate in eight weeks."

"That long?" I said.

"This is a government office. Promptness is not something we are known for."

"Or accuracy. I would hate to wait that long only to find out you sent me the wrong one. Can you pull it up on your computer and let me see it first?"

She grumbled, then stepped up to the computer. "I'll try."

After a few keystrokes, the woman perched her glasses on her nose and leaned in toward the screen. "Hm. The server is running slow."

"Is that a problem?" I asked.

She paused. "No."

Then she typed some more. "I'm showing an error locating your file. I'll have to cross-reference."

"Is that a problem?"

She paused. "No."

She typed again. "Ah! Here it is!"

"What does it say?" I asked impatiently.

"Interesting," she said, rubbing her chin. "Very interesting indeed."

"What is it?"

"This is highly unusual."

"Please, tell me what it says!"

She lowered her glasses and looked me in the eye. "I'm afraid I can't do that, miss," she said.

"Why not?"

"I'm not authorized to give out private information without my supervisor's approval, and he's at lunch."

What a rotten trick!

"Why didn't you tell me that at the beginning?" I asked.

"I repeat," she said, "you'll have your certificate in eight weeks. Good day!"

"Please let me see it. I won't tell anyone."

"Rules are rules, young lady. I wouldn't expect one so young as you to understand that."

I grabbed the computer monitor and turned it in my direction. But the instant it came into view . . .

Click!

That old witch cleared the screen.

Meeting Bob Phillips in the green city park was better than in a stuffy lawyer's office. The leaves in the maple trees showed off their fall colors. Birds sang happily from hundred-year-old oaks. Wooded paths meandered past fountains and a children's playground. It was cool and pleasant, and I felt relaxed—something I truly needed after dueling with that old biddy.

I sat on a park bench, where I told Bob to meet me. Directly in front of me stood a statue of Father Dorian. Fragrant flowers encircled the monument to our town's founding father. Dressed in his missionary robes, he held a dove in one hand, while the other reached up to heaven. A prankster had placed an empty liquor bottle in his raised hand. How appropriate.

Across the way was a shopping cart full of plastic garbage bags. Asleep on the bench next to it was a bag lady, huddled under a torn blanket. I remembered what Judge Higgins had said about homeless teenage runaways. Was I seeing my future self in that old woman?

"You wanted to see me?" said Bob Phillips. He took off his coat, slung it over his arm, and sat down on the bench next to me.

"Yes," I said. "How good are you at being a private eye?"

"I've never been one," said Bob, "nor would I want to be. What did you have in mind?"

"My mom has some information that I think has a bearing on my case. I need you to do some undercover work for me."

"I told you. I'm not a spy. I'm too old to play James Bond." He posed his fingers to look like a gun, then flashed me that raised, Sean Connery eyebrow.

"Don't be so dramatic," I said. "We're not talking international espionage. I think there may be some public records that will show what Mom is hiding from me. You're an attorney. You know how to get at that stuff."

Bob blew over the top of his index finger, as if his "hand" gun had just been fired. "I already know the information you're looking for."

"You do? Well, let's have it."

Bob stood up and put his coat back on. "Let's take a walk."

We strolled over to the playground. Children were laughing and playing, as all kids do when in the presence of seesaws, slides, and monkey bars.

"Give kids a place to play, and the real world disappears," said Bob. "Anything outside of their playground domain is of no concern. These kids don't even know we are watching them. The adult world, especially, is the farthest thing from their minds. The only thing that matters is how fast they can run, how high they can jump, and how loud they can scream."

"I guess that's true," I said, "but what are you getting at?"

"You may not want to hear this, but you're

somewhere between their world and adulthood. You still have one foot in the sandbox—and you should stay there."

"I get it," I said, feeling a bit insulted. "I'm not mature enough to be out in the adult world. I don't know what life is all about. Is that what you're saying?"

"Knowledge can be a dangerous thing if you're not equipped to handle it."

"Try me!"

Bob sat me down on a nearby bench.

"Families come in all shapes and sizes," he said. "Starting a family is a big step, and parents have a lot to consider before committing to it. Some want only a few children, some choose not to have any at all. But others dream of a big family. Your mom was one of those."

"I didn't know that," I said. "How many kids was she hoping for?"

"More than what she got. After delivering her last child, she learned that she was unable to have any more children."

"Oh, I see. Poor Mom. No wonder she won't talk about childbirth with me. She had my brother and sister, then I was born—and she probably blames me for not having the big family she always wanted."

"She doesn't blame you, Amy. You see, she only had two deliveries."

141

I suddenly realized what Bob was trying to tell me. "You're not going to say what I *think* you're going to say, are you?"

"I'm not suppose to tell you this, Amy." Bob swallowed hard. "You were adopted!"

I was in total shock. Somewhere out in the world were two important people I had never met: my *real* mom and dad.

"You mean I'm not Amy Dawson? Then who *am* I?"

"You know I can get disbarred for what I've told you already."

"The cat's out of the bag now, man. You *have* to tell me."

Bob took a deep breath.

"I've been in touch with my contact in the state records office. He has access to information that isn't available to the public. I told him about you, and asked him to do some digging into your past. He turned up records from an adoption agency confirming that your parents adopted a baby girl, around the same time you were born. He's trying to track down the adoption papers now, along with your original birth certificate, that will reveal your true birth mother's name. The certificate you have now was changed when you were adopted, naming your adoptive mom and dad as your parents. Due to privacy laws, adoptees are not permitted to see these documents, so I don't know how far we'll get."

"Are you sure about this?" I said.

"My sources are rock solid. It's all true."

My mind was whirling like a Texas tornado. This was too much to take in all at once. My whole world, not to mention my very existence, had been turned upside down. I found it hard to believe that Mom and Dad would keep the truth of my adoption hidden from me all these years. But then, I was living with impostors. What other lies were they keeping from me?

I was caught somewhere between confusion and rage.

Rage took over.

"There was another reason why I called this meeting with you," I told Bob. "I was seriously considering calling off this whole thing, but now I want it more than ever."

"Don't go there, Amy," said Bob. "Go back to that playground. Live in your own world however you imagine it, and leave the anguish of the mother who raised you outside. It's natural to blame her for not revealing your true past, but her decision to adopt you was made out of love."

"Ha! Love! You must be kidding. Now you listen to me, Mr. Family Law, I want this emancipation finalized. You hear me? I'll go anywhere the court sends me. Anything to get away from my lying parents!"

"If that's what you want," said Bob. "Just

remember this: whatever you think of your folks, they *chose* you to be part of their family. That's an extremely selfless thing to do for an orphan."

I had to admit, he had a point. Where would I be today if they hadn't taken me in? Still, there was a lot more to consider here.

"Okay," I said. "You can't blame me for being a little pissed, but I'll think it over."

"Good," said Bob. "And please don't tell anyone that we had this conversation."

"I promise. But you can't let my parents know that you talked to me, either. Deal?"

"Deal."

Then Bob started to walk off.

"Me and my big mouth," he said. "Some James Bond I would have made."

Chapter 14

Dad

*L*eaning against the front door jam of our house, Dad stretched the calf muscles in his legs—always a good idea before going for a run. On his doctor's orders, he was required to get some regular exercise. Too many idle hours in front of his big-screen TV had affected his health, and all that greasy popcorn had clogged his arteries like the sludge in a pig sty drain pipe.

I came down the stairs with my hair in a ponytail, wearing a Shankstonville High School t-shirt and purple gym shorts. It was a perfect, Sunday morning for getting in a little aerobic exercise—and to have a serious talk with my dad. My mission was to find out why my adoption was kept secret from me. Getting him alone might compel him to open up about it.

"I think I'll join you today," I said to my dad.

He was caught off guard by my forwardness. We

had hardly said a word to each other in months.

"You talking to me?" he said, checking to see if someone else was there. "I guess that'll be alright. But it won't be much of a workout. I don't go very fast."

"No matter."

Mom crossed the hallway with her morning cup of coffee, and spotted Dad and I talking. She came over to us, then looked me up and down as if she didn't know me. "What are you dressed up for?" she asked.

"Amy's coming with me," said Dad.

Then Mom straightened the collar on his Rolling Stones Tour t-shirt. "Alright, dear," she said. "But don't overdue it today. You're not running the Boston Marathon, you know."

She sipped her coffee, while giving me the evil eye over the rim of her cup. "You'll make sure he doesn't overdue it, won't you?" she said.

"S-sure thing, Mom." I said, hoping to avoid another confrontation with her.

"Well," said Dad. "Better get moving before I change my mind and sit down to *Good Morning America*."

I closed the front door behind us as Dad and I followed his usual routine: a pleasant jaunt downtown, then back home for a hearty breakfast.

Downtown Shankstonville wasn't too far from our house. Keeping to the sidewalk, my dad chugged along at a pretty good clip—better than I thought he would. I breezed along beside him without breaking a sweat.

"What made you decide to come?" asked Dad. "I thought you didn't want anything to do with me."

"I'm thinking about joining the cross-country team at school. Got to get into shape to make the cut."

"You sure that's the only reason?"

We were only two blocks from our house, and he already suspected that I had ulterior motives. He knew me all too well. This wasn't going to be as easy as I thought.

"A single girl in shorts running alone on the streets of Shankstonville isn't safe," I said. "These farmers might get the wrong idea."

Dad smiled.

We kept quiet for the next few blocks. Then it was time to get down to business.

"It just occurred to me," I said. "The last time we did anything like this, you were jogging behind a baby stroller, and I was in it."

"You were pretty easy to push back then," said Dad. "Small babies don't weigh very much."

"I didn't know I was that little. Was I premature or something?"

"No, just small. I can remember giving you your bottle and wondering which was bigger: you or the bottle."

"That must have been a plus for Mom. I mean, having me must have been a breeze."

Not surprisingly, Dad didn't reply.

"Remember that pink blanket you used to bundle me up in," I said, "the one with the embroidered rattles on it?"

"I remember," said Dad.

"I seem to recall that the hospital where I was born gave it to you. You told me once that I was so attached to it that I wouldn't let it go. Which hospital was that, anyway?"

Dad was spared from answering me by the approach of a rusty, old pickup truck. Straw spewed out behind it from the bails of hay in the cargo area. As it barreled up the street towards us, two young men riding in the cab waved their arms wildly out the windows.

"Hey, baby!" shouted one of the men, staring at me.

"Woo-hoo! Gimme some, darlin'!" whooped the other, waving his cowboy hat in the air.

In Shankstonville it was not uncommon for the locals to enjoy a beer or two before breakfast. These two acted like they had consumed an entire keg. Their truck swerved back and forth, crossing the center yellow line on the street repeatedly.

"How 'bout a kiss, sugar?"

"What ya doin' after school, sweetie?"

"Nice legs, girly!" they yelped.

I didn't feel the least bit threatened by those obnoxious, country hicks. Besides, I *did* have nice legs.

As the truck zoomed past us, I was surprised to see my dad flip them off, with an angry snarl on his face.

"Assholes!" he shouted at the brash young men.

I had to laugh.

"Hey, Dad," I said. "You handled that pretty well. I'm impressed."

"Ignorant hillbillies! People like that ought to be strung up by their—"

"You don't have to be so graphic, you know. Those kind don't bother me in the slightest."

"If you please, Amy, I'm trying to defend your honor."

"I can defend myself. I'm not some helpless damsel in distress. If I need a knight to rescue me, I'll call for one."

Dad didn't appreciate my sarcasm.

"Look, Amy," he said. "I know what you think of me. I haven't been the best father. You've made that abundantly clear. But that doesn't mean I don't care about you."

It had been a long time since I heard him express any kind of affection for me. I should have responded in kind, but I wasn't yet ready to be that forgiving.

We arrived in town and slowed to a walk, then

casually strolled past the shops along Hickory Street.

We stopped at the display window of Raintree Books, one of the last remaining independent bookstores in the county. Prominently displayed were stacks of my Dad's last novel, *Dawn of the Dworlocks:* an apocalyptic tale about a race of mutated lemurs that rule the Earth. It was his best-selling book to date. One of the books was turned around, showing my dad's smiling face on the back cover.

Just then, a man walked up and noticed the book in the window. He stared at the image on the back cover, then looked at my dad's face.

"Mornin', Mr. Dawson," said the man. Then he walked on.

"That's why I love it here," said Dad. "These country folk couldn't care less about celebrity."

Beside his novel was another stack of books —copies of my all-time favorite novel: *To Kill a Mockingbird.*

"Haven't read that one since high school," said Dad. "It was pretty good as I recall."

"Pretty good?" I said, shocked. "It's only the best book ever written!"

"The dad in that story had a funny name, I believe. Oh, yes, *Atticus Finch,* the devoted father."

"Don't forget *Scout,* the loving daughter."

"I remember Scout. She was *respectful* of her

father. An example every daughter should follow."

Dad glanced over at me to see if I had picked up on his not-so-subtle hint.

"And Atticus always told Scout the *truth*," I said. "A virtue all fathers should aspire to."

He wasn't expecting a comeback like that. As he considered my remark, I think he was starting to catch on to where I was going with all my needling.

We passed a sidewalk cafe. Customers sat at outdoor tables, leisurely enjoying their breakfasts in the fresh air.

"Speaking of good writing," said my dad, "here's a little trick I like to use when creating characters. I observe ordinary people, then imagine them in extraordinary situations. Take that couple, for example." He pointed out a young man and woman, gazing lovingly into each others eyes while sharing a chocolate eclair. "Young. Alive. Their life together filled with love and harmony. He's a married man, but that woman is not his wife. In exactly thirty seconds, his *real* wife will round the corner and find them together. Busted!"

Next to them sat an elderly couple, quietly sipping coffee. "Those two should be savoring their golden years together," said Dad. "But he suffers from dementia—at least that's what he's been told. She drugs his coffee every morning with a concoction that ravages his brain cells, while keeping the old man's bank book close to her."

Then came a man and woman with a small child. The parents were white. The child was black. I waited for Dad's take on this family, but he conveniently skipped over them.

"You missed one," I said.

"Did I?"

"Totally! They're a childless couple. The woman can't conceive, so they adopt. The baby is biracial, and light-skinned at birth. But the infant's complexion darkens as she gets older. The couple had planned to keep their adoption a secret, but must now face the music."

I studied my dad's face. If that little speech didn't get a confession out of him, nothing would. But he showed no emotion, as he stared off down the street.

"Time we started back," he said.

We picked up the pace and headed for home.

The run back was a quiet one. Dad had obviously grown tired of me questioning him, and had said all that he was going to say. But I still hadn't found the answers I was searching for.

"Ya know," I said, "I kinda like my story about the couple with the adopted baby. Maybe I'll write a short story about it."

"Almost home," said Dad, completely ignoring me. "I can smell our breakfast from here."

Time was running out.

"Don't change the subject," I said. "We were

talking about families with adopted children."

"You keep bringing up that subject of . . . you know what."

"Adoption? Why does it bother you to talk about it?

We looked over at each other for only an instant, but I could see the guilt in his eyes. I had broken through his defenses, and it was time for me to come clean.

"Why didn't you tell me?" I said.

"Tell you what?" Dad's voice was shaky.

"I know all about it. I was adopted, wasn't I?"

Dad's face turned pale. "W-why do you say that?"

"Don't try to deny it! I've been living in a house filled with lies, and you know it."

Dad staggered as his pace slowed. "We thought it would be better for you if nobody knew."

"You mean, better for *you!*"

Dad began sweating profusely, and his breathing became heavy. I grabbed his arm as his foot slipped off the edge of the curb.

"You okay, Dad?" I asked.

Just as we reached our house, he clutched his chest, then gasped for air as he fell to his knees. I watched in horror as his eyes rolled up into his head. Then he collapsed on his back onto the sidewalk.

Our front door swung open. Mom was standing

in the doorway. "Oh my God!" she screamed.

The front doors of our neighbor's homes flew open at my mom's shriek.

Mom rushed over to my dad, now lying unconscious, and cradled his head in her arms as she kneeled down beside him.

"What did you do to him?" she screamed at me.

"I know that you and dad adopted me, and I told him so."

My dad was now surrounded by our concerned neighbors. One man was on his knees giving him CPR.

Mom stood up to face me, her eyes glazed over with rage. "I wish we had left you behind at the orphanage!"

Tears were streaming down my cheeks. I bent down and grabbed Dad's wrist to check his pulse, but Mom yanked me back up.

"Don't you touch him," she yelled. Then she slapped my face so hard that I almost fell over. "You ungrateful little tramp! I'll be glad to be rid of you!"

I stood there shaking, as Mom returned to my dad's side.

I should have taken Bob's advice and stayed in that playground he so vividly described to me. I thought I could handle an adult situation, but I wasn't ready for it. I should have listened to Hubert, too, who told me I was screwing up a sweet deal with my boneheadedness. But most of all, I should have listened to Scout, who had the clearest message of all: respect your father, no matter what. Now, there was my dad, barely clinging to life, and my mom, wishing I was dead.

What was I going to do now?

Mom looked up at me. "Don't just stand there, damnit!" she said. "Call 9-1-1!"

Chapter 15

The Hospital

*T*he smell of fresh-cut carnations freshened the air in the hospital waiting area. Vinyl-upholstered chairs sat along the walls, under religious paintings of biblical figures I did not recognize. People waited patiently, reading newspapers or being entertained by their mobile devices. Some waited to be treated for an illness or injury. Others waited to visit their afflicted loved ones. It was early evening, and I was there to see Dad.

A female receptionist stood behind a circular desk, placing long-stemmed roses in a tall vase.

"Hello," I said to her, in a respectful, low voice.

"You don't have to speak softly here," she said. "This isn't a library."

"But everyone else is."

"That's because they're either worried, bereaved, or in pain. What can I help you with?"

"I wonder if you can direct me to the patient's ward."

"Why? Are you sick?"

"No, it's my dad. He was admitted this morning, and I want to see him."

"I see. You're the worried type." She pointed to a pair of swing doors across the room. "Go through there. To your left you'll see the nurses station. They can tell you where to go from there."

"Thanks."

Check In Here read the sign over the nurses station. Medics in sterile facemasks and doctors in surgical gowns scurried about, like commuters in a subway station. The sounds of TV game shows and sporting events trickled out of the patient's rooms, as I approached the counter.

A woman in a white nurses cap greeted me.

"Good evening," she said pleasantly. "How may I help you?"

"I'm trying to locate a hospital room."

"Why? Are you sick?"

"No. I'm looking for my father."

The nurse sat down at her computer. "The patient's name, please."

"Dawson," I said.

"And you are?"

"Amy."

As she stared at the screen, her eyes suddenly widened. "Oh, dear," she said.

"What is it?" I asked. "Is something wrong?"

She put her hands on her hips and looked at me with disgust. "It says here that your Dad suffered a heart attack due to complications brought on by a self-centered, teenage daughter. That wouldn't be you, would it?"

"That's not what it says," I insisted, making light of her remark.

She clicked her mouse. "He also suffers from an acute case of Cardiac Sorebosis."

"What's that?"

"A broken heart."

"I didn't ask you for his diagnosis, Nurse. I just want to know which room he's in."

"Very well," she sighed. "Go down this corridor and take a right past the infant care nursery. He's in room 112."

I didn't bother with a *"thank you"* to the sassy nurse.

I walked briskly down the corridor, then slowed down, as I began to consider what I was doing there. For sure, I was worried about my dad, but I selfishly wanted to clear my own conscience, too. We all knew Dad had a heart condition, but the nurse was right to blame me for him now being hospitalized. There was a far more disturbing fact, however, one that was brutally tearing my heart apart. Not all people survive heart attacks.

I came to a full stop in front of the nursery,

having second thoughts about being in the hospital at all. Then I looked through the nursery window at the babies inside. Rows of hospital cribs filled the room, each holding a single newborn. Only a few babies were crying, while the rest of them slept peacefully in the climate-controlled space.

A name was attached to each crib, identifying the baby inside.

I saw Albert: 7 lbs, 6oz.

Bernice: 8 lbs, 3oz.

and Amy!

What a coincidence. A baby with the same name as mine. Then I noticed that the crib was empty. She must be out for her evening feeding, I thought. No, that must be her being bottle-fed by that person in the corner.

In a rocking chair sat a man, with a tiny baby in his arms. He rocked gently, back and forth, while bottle-feeding the precious infant. Such care.

Wait a minute!

I pressed my face to the glass. The pink blanket that covered the baby had rattles embroidered on it. I knew that blanket like I knew my own skin. That was *my* blanket!

I banged on the glass. "Hey, you!" I yelled, but the man didn't look up. I dashed around the corner to the nursery entrance and swung open the door.

"What the hell's going on here?" I shouted.

But instead of hearing the sounds of crying

babies, I entered to the shouts of *"Happy Birthday!"* Where the cribs had been was now a kitchen table. Helium balloons on ribbons rose from a colorful centerpiece, next to a birthday cake with five burning candles on top. A small group of people in party hats cheered as the same man I saw through the glass entered, with a little girl in a pink dress clinging to his shoulders.

After a rousing chorus of "Happy Birthday to You," the man sat the little girl down in front of the cake. "Happy birthday, Amy," he said to her. The man was my father, 11 years younger, and I was the 5-year-old being honored.

The scene played out exactly as I remembered it. I watched in stunned silence as my past was replayed before my eyes. No one seemed to be aware of my presence. I was Mr. Scrooge being shown his former life by the *Ghost of Christmas Past*.

"Now make a wish, Amy, and blow out the candles," said my dad, "but don't tell anybody what it is, or it might not come true."

"Can I tell *you?*" asked little Amy, in a sweet voice.

"Well, okay. I'll make an exception this time."

Dad leaned down as the girl whispered softly in his ear. No one heard what she was saying, but I remember exactly what I told him that day: *I wish we will always be together.*

The birthday girl in the pink dress blew out her

candles, with a little help from her proud father.

Everyone applauded, and I would have clapped along with them, had I not been wiping the tears from my eyes. Seeing my dad's sweetness, knowing how horribly I had treated him that morning was more than I could stand.

I couldn't get out of there fast enough. I raced out the door, only to find myself in another room. The sounds of the party abruptly stopped the instant the door slammed shut behind me.

The space was pitch black and dead quiet. Suddenly, a row of light panels on the wall came on, lighting up the empty room. The panels were those illuminated displays doctors use to look at x-rays. But these weren't revealing some sick patient's skeletal innards, they were playing old home videos from my past.

Each panel showed a different stage of my life growing up with my parents. The deeply personal moments included me as a 3-year-old, climbing into bed with my dad during a lightning storm; baking oatmeal cookies with my mom when I was 7; getting kissed on the forehead by both of them at my junior high school graduation.

The volume of the soundtracks steadily increased the longer I stayed in the room. I held my hands over my ears as the sound got louder, finally merging into a mish-mash of noise that I couldn't bear to listen to.

With my eardrums about to burst, I opened the door into another room. I was in a darkened hallway. Moonlight streamed in through a window, left open to a wintry night. I knew that window, having spent many hours gazing up at the stars through it. I was in the hall outside my bedroom, in the city apartment I knew as a child.

I crept carefully into the familiar scene, as fond memories of those happy times came flooding back to me. Then I heard the latch of my bedroom door. Our family doctor was quietly closing it as he stepped into the hallway. He tip-toed right past me without saying a word, like I was invisible.

Reaching for the doorknob, I opened it ever so slowly, and peered inside my room. Under the light of my nightstand lamp, I saw 10-year-old Amy, laying silently under the covers of her bed, with a damp washcloth across her forehead. Kneeling on the floor beside her was my dad, his hands clasped together in prayer. Tears ran down his cheeks as he bowed his head in silence.

I remember that night, suffering with a raging fever, but through my delirium, had no memory of my dad being in the room with me. I had contracted a grave illness, that I later learned I had barely lived through.

I never realized that the trials of parenting could be so profound. For sure, seeing these past events from a fresh point-of-view was eye-opening. But I was now filled with remorse for not being more understanding. If only I had known.

I started to walk toward my grieving father with my outstretched hand, when the lamp suddenly went out, leaving the room in total darkness.

A light faded up behind me. As I spun around, I was now in a hospital patient room. The walls were bare and the room was empty, save a single bedside curtain. I heard the faint beeping of a heart monitor and the mechanical noise of a breathing apparatus. The light behind the translucent partition projected the silhouette of someone lying in a hospital bed.

I pulled back the curtain. There in the bed lay my dad, in a coma, an oxygen mask over his mouth. IV fluids dripped down narrow tubes to needles inserted in his arms.

I walked around the side of the bed and stood over him, then took hold of his hand. I wanted to tell him how awful I felt, how I wish I could take back all the suffering I had caused him. But I was unable to speak. Even if I could, he probably wouldn't hear me anyway.

On the night table lay a copy of *To Kill a Mockingbird*. I picked it up and gently glided my fingers over the cover, like it was made of fine silk.

I held the book close to my face.

"Are you in there, Scout?" I said. "What do I tell him? I have so much to say, but can't find the words. The funny thing is, I've never been at a loss for words before. That's part of my problem, you see. I talk when I should be listening. You always listened to Atticus whenever there was a crisis. Now I'm facing the biggest crisis in my life. Tell me what to do."

The flashing lights of the machines were blurred through the tears in my eyes. My fingers tightened around the book.

"What am I doing?" I cried, throwing the book down on the table. "Why am I talking to you, Scout? You're nothing but a fictional character, hatched out of someone's fantasy. This is reality. Go back! You don't belong here!"

I marched out of the room and slammed the door behind me, then leaned against it with my head in my hands. The bustling sounds of a busy hospital returned. Looking up, I was back in the hospital corridor.

I was emotionally exhausted. Dragging myself back to the nurses station, I walked up to the same nurse I had spoken to earlier.

She smiled at me. "How can I help you?"

"I need a drink of water," I said.

"Why? Are you sick?"

"I'm tired and I'm thirsty. No one should have to go through what I just did."

"Did you find your father?"

"I found that I'm a terrible person who should be put away before she hurts anyone else."

"That's good!" said the nurse, bubbling over with enthusiasm. She reached over and felt my forehead with the palm of her hand.

"Yup," she said. "The fever's broken. I think you're okay to go home now."

I pushed her hand away. "What's the matter with you people?" I shouted. The entire hospital staff stopped and stared at me from my outburst. "Everyone keeps asking me if I'm sick. I ask for simple directions, and instead you send me on a magical mystery tour. I came here to talk to my dad, and I couldn't even do that. Now you tell me to go home. What kind of a hospital is this?"

The nurse grabbed the base of her neck and lifted upward. A rubber mask rolled over her face to reveal the head of a *sheep* underneath it. The rest of the hospital workers pulled masks off of their heads, too. There were *tiger* doctors, *panda* interns, and *monkey* orderlies.

"I knew it!" I said in a fit of anger. "Fritterz! This is a fake hospital!"

"Not really," said the sheep nurse. "Hospitals are institutions of healing. Sick and anguished people go there when they have nowhere else to turn. They beg for a cure, but sometimes the best medicine is already inside them. You came here to find a sick patient. You just didn't know that patient was *you.*"

"Where's my dad!" I shouted.

"In the hands of medical science—and God. Go home, Amy. There's nothing more you can do for him."

I ran to the doors that led to the waiting area, then looked back at the Fritterz. They stared at me in silence, then slowly faded away like ghosts, as the human hospital staff faded in, going about their normal duties.

I pushed through the doors, plopped down in a chair, and folded my arms. I was pissed!

A woman seated next to me was reading a newspaper, with a large photo on the front page. It showed President Kennedy's young son saluting a flag-draped casket, following his father's assassination. The headline read *Nation Prepares for Kennedy Remembrance*. I felt little John, Jr.'s anguish, not knowing if my own father would survive the night.

The woman saw me studying her paper. "A tragic day," she said to me. "No one should lose their father at such a young age. But no one saw it coming."

I had to agree with her. How could anyone have predicted we would suffer our country's greatest loss on that fateful day in *1963!*

Kennedy was shot on November 22nd. Today was November 20th.

Maybe no one on that day 50 years ago could do anything to prevent it.

But *I* could!

Chapter 16

Saving Kennedy

*T*he blast of the train's steam whistle could be heard all over Theme Farm. The old train was a throwback to the ones from the 19th century that took presidential candidates on whistle-stop tours all over America. Red, white, and blue banners adorned the platform behind the rear passenger car. From there, ambitious candidates would address cheering crowds at station stopovers.

Theme Farm's train only circled the perimeter of the park. It was dubbed *The Washington Express*—so named because it just goes around and around, and never gets anywhere. It seemed appropriate that Hubert and I should be riding this presidential relic, since we were there to discuss preventing President Kennedy's assassination.

Since the day I first met Clifford, Hubert had respected my privacy, never once pressing me to include him in my Used-to-Be TV adventures.

While I kept the personal side of my activities to myself, the plot to save Kennedy needed to be thoroughly thought out, and I welcomed Hubert's input.

He had compiled the historical facts of the event and organized them on his tablet. It showed all the pertinent information, along with news film footage. An animated map detailed the location and timing of everything that happened that day.

The assassination occurred at 12:30 pm. President Kennedy was riding in a motorcade through downtown Dallas, when his assassin fired at him from the sixth-floor window of a building along the route.

"I don't know if saving Kennedy is possible," said Hubert, "I've analyzed the data, and haven't come up with a foolproof approach that won't endanger Clifford. If he tells the police what's going to happen, they'll lock him up as a terrorist. Then when he fails to stop it, he'll be implicated in the murder. Telling the cops who the gunman is won't help, either, because the perpetrator can't be arrested without probable cause. Even if he wants to physically protect the President, he'll never get past the Secret Service. You got any ideas?"

"Yes," I said. "No weapon—no assassination."

"Huh?"

"It's simple. Kennedy was shot with a high-powered rifle. We know how and when his killer will smuggle his weapon into the building. All Clifford has to do is disarm him before he gets there."

"That'll mean confronting a deranged and dangerous killer. Doesn't that bother you?"

"For sure. But Clifford's a big time, political activist now. He won't shy away from a chance like this."

Hubert closed his tablet. "I don't know, Amy. Something feels wrong about this. If it works, you will have saved a great man and altered history, but you may be changing more than you know."

"I'll be changing things for the *better.*"

"Don't be so sure. Lyndon Johnson only became president as a direct result of the assassination. He might never have been president had Kennedy lived. It was LBJ who signed the Civil Rights Act—*not* Kennedy. We might see separate "white" and "colored" drinking fountains at school if this works."

"But what about Vietnam? It was *Johnson* who escalated the war. Kennedy might have pulled our troops out had he not been killed. Clifford would like that."

The train bell rang as it rolled in to the station. The conductor called out: "Attention all passengers! Disembark here for these attractions: The Sweet Revenge Bakery, Hall of Wartime Presidents, and *Used-to-Be TV.*"

The old locomotive came to a stop. "This is where I get off," I said.

I stepped off the train, then waved to Hubert as the engine's big wheels started to turn.

Hubert leaned out the window.

"Don't do this, Amy!" he begged me. "You're messing with something more powerful than you know."

The train picked up speed and rounded the bend out of sight, on to its next stop.

I knew exactly what Hubert was trying to tell me, but I didn't care. How often have people debated what they would change if they could go back in time? The classic scenario is to go to 1930s Germany and take out Hitler. Who hasn't wished that were possible? But I wasn't trying to kill anybody. I wanted to *save* someone, and ensure that those Kennedy kids would live a long life with their father. What better motive could there be than that?

I made sure that I had Hubert's tablet with me as I locked the door to my cottage. If I was going to try to save Kennedy, I could immediately confirm my success or failure by searching online resources

I turned on the tablet, then checked—and double-checked—the strength of the WiFi signal. This was no time for a technical glitch.

While I waited for Clifford, I searched: *Kennedy Assassination.* The results showed the details as they currently existed. The images from that November were almost too hard to look at: the disbelief in the faces of those who witnessed the shooting; the throngs of mourners filing past the casket; Kennedy's young family saying their final goodbyes. It all reinforced my commitment to reverse this brutal and unnecessary tragedy.

One website showed the headlines from all the major newspapers on that sad day. All I had to do was refresh the tablet display, and if anything had changed, the headlines would reflect it.

I heard someone enter the security office on the TV.

"It's about time," I said. But it wasn't Clifford sitting down in the chair, it was his dad, Earl! Sarah was with him.

"Oh, hello Mr. and Mrs. Anderson," I said. "I didn't expect to see you."

"We'd like to speak with you alone," said Earl.

"Is everything okay? Is Clifford alright?"

"That's a matter of opinion," said Sarah. "His health is fine, if that's what you're asking, but his head is a little messed up."

I knew right away why Sarah was upset. Clifford was not the same person I met three months earlier. His political views had put him at odds with his folks, and I feared he might have done something to turn his parents against him.

"Is Clifford there?" I asked timidly.

"Forget about Clifford for a moment," grumbled Earl. "It's *you* I'm angry with. You see this?" He held up Clifford's Selective Service papers, ripped to shreds. The little pieces had been taped back together. "Clifford did this right in front of us, just to make us mad. It's not like him."

"I'm sorry," I said. "Can I talk to Clifford, now?"

"You may not!" shouted Earl. "I blame *you* for this. He used to be a sensible, patriotic young man before he met you. Now it's, '*Amy* wouldn't put up with your crap,' or '*Amy* could teach you a thing or two.'"

"That's not my fault."

"He skips school to go to protest rallies. His grades are so appalling that he won't be graduating from high school this year."

"I had nothing to do with that."

"You've been a bad influence on him, Amy. You put ideas in his head and turned him into one of those radical troublemakers."

It was time I stood up for myself.

"I didn't do any such thing!" I yelled. "Just because you can't control your own son is no fault of mine."

"You see?" said Sarah. "That's just the attitude we're talking about. No respect."

Arguing with Clifford's parents felt just like fighting with my own, and I didn't like it. I cooled down and took a deep breath.

"I don't mean to sound disrespectful," I said. "You're good parents. I knew that the first time I met you. But you have to accept part of the blame for Clifford's rebelliousness. You question his patriotism because his love-of-country doesn't include dying in a jungle war. You expect him to follow in your footsteps instead of letting him find his own path. Blame me if you want, but Clifford and his generation are already heading down that road, with no help from me."

Earl had calmed down by now, too. "There is some truth in what you say. Please understand. We're only interested in Clifford's well-being."

"Then permit me to offer you one piece of advice. Talk to him. Try to see the world through his eyes. Communicating is everything. That's a lesson I learned a little too late. If you really love your son, you'll give him that much consideration."

"It's not that simple," said Earl. "Clifford's a legal adult now, and I can't force him to do anything he doesn't want to. But I still have some control over his life, and I'm going to use it. I'm disconnecting this video equipment. You won't be seeing Clifford again. I'll give you five minutes to say goodbye."

I was devastated, but what could I do? Reach through the screen and stop him from pulling the plug? Earl's mind was made up and that was that. But his actions were not going to stop me from accomplishing my mission.

As Earl and Sarah walked out of frame, Clifford entered and slumped down in the chair.

"What was all that about?" he asked, adjusting his shades.

"Never mind," I said. "We don't have much time. Can your mom and dad hear us?"

"They've left the room. What is it?"

"What I am about to say is extremely important. I need to ask a favor of you. It involves President Kennedy."

"A fine man. What's your favor?"

"He's going to be assassinated tomorrow."

Clifford quickly sat up and removed his shades. "That's crazy. He's one of the most beloved presidents we've ever had. Are you sure about this?"

"I know the future, remember? How would you like to save his life?"

Clifford fell back into his chair. "You think I can? It sounds kinda dangerous."

"Not if you do as I say."

I explained the facts to Clifford: the presidential motorcade in Dallas, the manner in which it will be done, the who, when, and how.

"What do I have to do?" asked Clifford.

"Listen close. The assassin's name is Lee Harvey Oswald. He looks like this." I held up a picture of his police mugshot. "Tomorrow morning he will be driven to work carrying a long, paper package. He'll tell everybody there are curtain rods inside, but it's really a rifle. He'll be dropped off in front of the building at 7:23. Just look for a black, 1954 Chevrolet Bel Air. All you have to do is grab that package away from him before he enters the building. He won't suspect a thing."

"Whoa, man. This is heavy."

I could see Clifford starting to sweat, even in black and white.

"Think about this: what you do could very well change the course of the Vietnam War. You might not have to go, if this works."

I looked down and refreshed the screen on my tablet. The headlines hadn't changed.

"I don't know, Amy," said Clifford. "This is kind of wiggin' me out. I'm all for changing the world, and all, but this . . ."

"Well, here's your big chance. You're the only one who knows what's going to happen. You *have* to do this."

"But what will this do to *your* time? Have you thought about that? Everything will change for you, too."

"I know that. But isn't saving a life—especially of someone this important—worth it?"

Suddenly, I heard a loud banging on the window behind me.

"Stop, Amy!" screamed a voice.

It was Hubert.

"What's going on there?" said Clifford. "Who's

that yelling?"

I hit the refresh button again with my shaking finger. The headlines were still the same.

No . . . wait!

They *weren't* the same!

While the bold headlines hadn't changed, I had neglected to notice the subheadings:

"Brave Teen Dies in Bold Attempt to Save Kennedy."

Clifford had indeed confronted Kennedy's assassin. Apparently, he missed his chance to engage Oswald on the street. He found his way to the 6th floor, moments before the fatal shots were fired, and tried to wrestle the rifle away from the shooter. But the older, stronger Oswald mortally wounded Clifford. Oswald then aimed his sites on the presidential motorcade, and killed his victim exactly as it happened.

Clifford was pronounced dead at the hospital shortly afterward.

Hubert was now ramming his shoulder against the cottage door, trying to break it down.

I looked up at Clifford in a panic.

"Clifford!" I shouted. "Listen to me! Don't—"

But the TV suddenly went black.

Silence.

"Cliff?"

There was no response.

I held my hand over my mouth as my eyes filled with tears. "Oh, no!" I whimpered. "Dear God!"

I clicked on a link in one of the online articles. News photos showed Clifford on an ambulance stretcher, being wheeled out of the building.

Hubert finally burst through the door.

I ran to him and threw my arms around his neck, crying hysterically.

"Amy!" said Hubert. "Are you alright?"

"I killed them!" I said, sobbing. "I killed them both."

"I know. I was monitoring the news from that year, when I saw the reports change. I'm sorry."

Hubert and I slowly walked to the door. A group of onlookers stood in the doorway and gawked at us.

Then a Theme Farm security guard forced his way through the crowd.

"Sorry, folks," he said. "This attraction is now closed. Please enjoy the many other shows the park has to offer."

"What happened?" Hubert asked the guard.

"Looks like they've lost the signal to 1963 for good," he said. "That happens sometimes."

I turned and took one last look at the dark TV screen.

"Goodbye, Cliff," I said in a whisper.

Out in the daylight, Hubert sat me down on a bench by a tranquil lake. A beautiful water fountain erupted from the middle of it.

"I should have listened to you," I told Hubert. "I should have left history the way it was. Instead, I got an innocent boy killed. All I wanted to do was reverse the evil that mankind does to himself."

Hubert wrapped his arm around my shoulder. "We all wish we could do that," he said.

"But I had *more* than a wish." I reached into my pocket and pulled out the magic clicker. "I had the solution right here in my hand."

"I guess some things are just meant to be."

I held the tablet up and hit the play button on the video file I had made of Clifford.

"Sure I have. It's a baseball card binder."

"Not all things," I said. "Maybe nothing could have prevented Kennedy's death, but Clifford wasn't meant to die at 18."

Then I stood up, and with all my might flung the clicker into the middle of the lake.

Chapter 17

The Letter

I stared out at the highway ahead of me, heartsick, while Hubert drove me home. My tears were dry and my mind was clear, but I still couldn't come to terms with having sent Clifford off to his death.

Hubert thought that talking about it would make me feel better.

"What's done is done," he said. "No sense in dwelling on what can't be changed. By the next time we visit Theme Farm, you'll have forgotten all about it."

"I never want to go back to that place again," I said.

"You can't do that. What about me? It won't be the same going in there without you. Besides, you'll miss the opening of the new ride, *The Carousel of Regression*. It's a musical tribute to the de-evolution of humankind."

"*De*-evolution is right. Humanity is going backwards. We should have risen above killing each other to get what we want by now, but it's just as true today as it was in '63. We'll all be living in caves before you know it."

"You could be right. Fortunately, there are a few brave souls around to show that there is still hope for us—like you and Clifford. I've never seen such courage in anyone. Take some comfort in that, Amy. You've earned it."

"And what did poor Clifford earn?"

Hubert had no answer for that.

Our drive home took us past the Jiffy Fizz Cola plant. Giant renderings of their iconic, blue cans were painted on the side of it.

"I still can't believe those cans used to be red," said Hubert. "But they're blue now, and I guess it'll have to stay that way. With the time portal closed, there's no way to reach Clifford to ask him to change it back—this is, if we could go back *before*. . . you know what I mean."

I knew exactly what Hubert meant: you can't communicate with the dead. Clifford was gone, and his memory was all that remained.

"Slow down," I told Hubert, as we passed the old building. Clifford had known it when it was nothing more than a concrete slab. I wondered if his initials were still in the cement where he had written them as a mischievous boy. His letter of apology could still be tucked into the wall, for all I knew, waiting to be discovered.

Waiting to be discovered! That gave me an idea.

"Maybe we can't reach Clifford," I said, "but maybe *he* can still reach us. Turn around!"

"What for? Where are we going?"

"The Jiffy Fizz plant. There may be a letter there for me, postmarked 50 years ago."

We drove up a long driveway that led to the historic building. The grounds were deserted. It was the weekend, and there probably weren't many people on the job.

Ahead of us was a security checkpoint, and beyond its open gate, the plant's main entrance. As we got closer, an imposing security guard stepped out of a small guard shack.

"What do we say to that guard?" asked Hubert.

"Tell him you have to use the bathroom," I said. "Tell him it's an emergency."

"That's not gonna work. He's not going to let us through unless we can prove we have business inside."

"Tell him I'm the boss's daughter, and I'm here to see Da-da."

"Be serious."

"Then *you* think of something."

We slowed down as the guard approached us. Hubert came to a stop and rolled down the window.

"Good afternoon, sir," said the burly guard. "Do you have an appointment?"

Hubert gulped. "Well, not exactly."

"You need an appointment before I can let you in. Is there someone I can call for you?"

"Yes . . . I mean, no . . . I mean . . . can I use your bathroom?"

"What?"

"It's an emergency."

"I think you'd better turn around and leave, son."

Hubert pointed to the passenger seat. "But this is the boss's . . ." But the seat was empty. While Hubert had distracted the guard, I quietly slipped out the door and crept toward the building without him seeing me.

I hid behind a tall hedge growing against the wall by the front entrance. There was just room enough between the wall and the foliage for me to move around. As I inched toward the front door, I brushed aside the dirt and dry leaves at my feet to expose the building's concrete footing. Suddenly, there it was! Etched into the concrete surface were the initials *C.A.*—Clifford Anderson!

I guided my fingers up the wall directly above them, looking for the gap between the bricks Clifford had told me about. I found it about 18 inches up, and felt inside with my fingertips. Something was definitely in there. Using my fingernails like tweezers, I pulled out a piece of paper wrapped in plastic—weathered, but intact.

After blowing off the dust, I opened one end, then very carefully slid out the paper. I unfolded what appeared to be standard binder paper, though yellowed with age. From the handwriting, it clearly was *not* Clifford's boyhood apology. Then came my reward for my snoopiness. It was a letter from Clifford . . . written to me!

This is what it said:

November 22, 1963

Dear Amy,

It's 5:00 AM, and I am about to leave for the bus station. There I will catch a ride to Dallas, even though I'm not quite sure why I'm doing it. What you told me about Kennedy was so fantastic that I'd be foolish not to at least investigate. I don't know what I will find when I get there, but I'm going to follow your plan and see what happens.

Telling me what you did took a lot of courage. That's one of the things I like best about you. There are a lot more nice things I could say, but they are too numerous to list here. It's funny how easy it is to tell you things. I've never felt so comfortable around anyone.

I don't know if I will ever talk to you again. The TV went blank before I had a chance to say goodbye. But I wrote this song last night, and it probably best describes how I feel:

Goodbye, sweet melody
You were my friend from the start
And though I'll never see your face again
Your song stays in my heart.

So long, sweet melody
You came to me in a dream
and showed me just how lonely I have been
And what a life in love can mean.

Sweet melody
Our song had just begun
As sweet a song as anyone can play
As sweet a song as anyone can play.

Well, I gotta go. I'll put this letter in the wall at Jiffy Fizz, in hopes that you will find it 50 years from now. That sounds like such a long time, but they say that love is timeless.

Did I say love?

Yes, Amy, I did!

Goodbye, Sweet Melody.

Cliff

I neatly folded Clifford's letter and put it in my pocket.

Back at the gate, I saw Hubert's car, still parked at the guard shack with the engine running. The guard was inside talking on the phone. I sprinted to the car and flung open the passenger-side door, just as the guard hung up.

"Hit it!" I told Hubert.

The engine raced.

"Hey!" shouted the guard, as we sped off in reverse. "You come back here!"

I leaned my head out the car window and shouted at him, "I'm telling Da-da on you!"

Please Pardon Our Dust read the sign in front of the Used-to-Be TV attraction. A tall barrier had been erected around the building, hiding the messy construction site from park guests. Under cover of darkness, I found an opening between the wall's plywood sheets, just big enough for me to squeeze through. Hubert kept a watchful eye out for security guards and curious spectators. Then he signaled me that it was safe to duck inside.

Work lights lit up the attraction's neighborhood set, revealing the false building fronts and hollow props, typical of what you would find on a movie soundstage. Seeing it kind of destroyed the illusion of a quaint, residential street in the 1960s at dusk. The sunset was only a painted wall. Audio speakers that played night sounds hung from the rafters.

The door stood open to the cottage where I had

spent so much time visiting with Clifford. I crept inside the eerie, dark space. The swag lamp was off. The harsh light outside sliced through the blackness as it streamed in through the window.

I sat down on the couch and stared at the TV, as if it would magically come to life at any moment, with Clifford on the screen waiting for me.

I wasn't quite sure why I felt compelled to return to that place. The sudden breakdown of the attraction was like having a podium mic fail in the middle of a speech. I had been cut off when there was still so much more to be said. Now I wanted the last word.

"Hey, Cliff," I said to the blank screen. "I got your letter. Thanks for saying all those nice things. I love your new song lyrics. They'll fit right in with all the great music that's coming your way. You're gonna love The Beatles. It's going to be such a wonderful time to be young.

I kneeled down in front of the TV to get closer.

"I know you can't hear me, Cliff. Forgive my foolishness, but letting go of someone you care so much about isn't an easy thing to do. I can still see you right here in front of me. I can see that silly yo-yo you were so attached to before you invited me into your world—a world we shared in the same space, separated only by time."

I touched the screen, slowly running my fingers down the cold glass. Then I placed my cheek against it.

"Yes, Cliff, it *was* love—as pure and honest as any two people can experience. No one should go through life without sharing that precious gift."

I stood up.

"Well, I have to go now. I'm glad we had this chat, even though it was a little one-sided."

I stood there for moment, as if Clifford was about to speak to me, but the TV lay silent. I placed my hand on the top of it one last time and bowed my head, then turned and faced the door.

I didn't look back as I left the cottage.

I pried apart the barrier outside the attraction, and reentered the park where Hubert was waiting for me.

"You okay, Amy?" he said. "What's it like in there?"

"Depressing," I said. "Like going to a funeral with a TV set instead of a coffin."

"Are you sorry you did it?"

"Not really. I think I'm ready to put the past behind me now. It's time I started living in the present."

"*Theme Farm is now ending its normal operating day,*" said a voice over the park's PA system.

As Hubert and I exited the park, I looked up at the moon. It was full and bright, and lit up the ground like a gigantic street lamp. Was Clifford's face up there looking down on me? No, and I don't suppose it ever did. That was just a sentimental whim that Clifford dreamed up out of his imagination. I loved sharing that fantasy with him. But like a dream that melts away with the dawn, it was time for me to wake up.

Chapter 18

The Ruling

A fly landed on the judge's bench, buzzing its wings as it crawled onto my emancipation papers. I had seen a fly just like it on my first day in that courtroom, clinging to a window, hoping for an escape. That fly was smart enough to avoid human contact. This one wasn't. The judge had come prepared this time to deal with the pesky fly. He picked up a fly-swatter, and in an instant the little pest was flattened. That fly and I shared the same dream to be free. My own prospects for independence were not looking good. Bring on the Amy-swatter.

All I wanted was the right to make my own decisions, to live where I wanted and with whomever I pleased. Having received my parents' blessing, it should have been a slam-dunk, but my attorney warned me not to expect a favorable outcome. My climb to freedom was feeling more like a convict's last mile to imprisonment. All that remained was for the judge to hand down his sentence.

Bob Phillips and I sat at the attorneys table. My hands were folded in my lap as Judge Higgins began to speak.

"This should have been an open-and-shut case," he said. "Emancipation of a Minor, while rare, is not a complicated request. What has become an issue, in this case, is where Amy will live afterwards. She has voiced her vehement disapproval of being placed in foster care, and if so ordered, threatens to runaway. Such an action on her part may lead to dire consequences, of which she is fully aware. The burden now lies with the court to decide what is best for her."

Here it comes, I thought. My hands were gripped so tightly together that I had cut off the blood flow to my fingertips.

"Therefore," concluded the judge, "I am ordering that Amy be remanded to the Shankstonville Juvenile Correction Facility, where she will remain until alternative housing can be provided, or until she comes of legal age."

I jumped to my feet. "You can't do this!" I yelled.

"I'm sorry," said the judge, "but you leave me no alternative." Then he picked up a pen and started to seal my fate with his signature.

I turned to Bob. "Do something!" I shouted.

"What kind of attorney are you?"

Bob rose to his feet. "If it pleases the court . . ."

There was a long pause. The judge held his pen in the air, waiting to hear Bob's argument.

"I object!"

"On what grounds, counselor," asked the judge.

"On the grounds that this hearing is not yet concluded." He pulled some papers from his briefcase. "New information has been brought to my attention that may impact your decision. I offer into evidence, these documents: Amy's adoption papers and her original birth certificate."

I had misjudged Bob. He was like the state governor in those old crime movies, who grants a stay of execution to a prisoner in his final hour. He was taking an awful risk, though. Those documents had been obtained illegally, and producing them could very well mean that he will never practice law again.

"These documents," said Bob, handing them to the judge, "suggest that there may yet be a blood relative, very much alive, and willing to take custody of Amy."

Judge Higgins examined the papers. "Yes, this does change things. But wait! This birth certificate only shows *Amy* as her first name. No last name was recorded."

Now what? Things were just starting to go my way, and I wasn't in the mood for another setback.

I marched up to the bench and ripped the paper from the judge's hands. There it was: *Amy,* with my last name left blank, along with my weight, length, time of birth, and all that. Then I saw my birth mother's name. It was Mary Ruth *Phillips.*

I shot a scathing look over at Bob. "What is this?" I said. "My mother's last name is the same as yours."

Bob reached into his briefcase and pulled out the photo I had seen on his desk—the vacation snapshot of him and a young woman.

"You once asked me who was in this picture with me," he said. "It's your mother."

"How is that possible?" I said.

"Because your mother . . . was my daughter."

My shock left me speechless while I pieced together all that I had just heard.

"Let me get this straight. If that woman is my mother, and my mother is *your* child, then that makes you . . ."

"Exactly. I'm your *grandfather!*"

Bob placed more documents before the judge.

"Here is my sworn statement, your honor," said Bob. "I married in 1973, and shortly after, we were blessed with a beautiful, baby daughter. We named her Mary. At 25 she became pregnant. She was a single woman, and we never learned who the father was. In 1998, she gave birth to a healthy, baby girl. Tragically, complications developed during delivery, and Mary died giving life to her daughter."

Bob paused to look at the framed photo, then continued:

"As Mary's father, and her only living relative, I was awarded guardianship of my grandchild. I had been widowed some time earlier, and with my child-rearing days well behind me, I decided to put her up for adoption—with the stipulation that she keep the name her mother had chosen for her: Amy."

Bob returned the photo to his briefcase. "And that's not all."

Then he began to sing a song, very faintly at first:

"Your love, like music . . ."

I gasped. "Where did you learn that song?"

". . . Like sweet melodies . . ."

I slammed my fist on the table. "Your honor, I want a new attorney!"

". . . Dancing on the keys of my piano."

I walked up to Bob and was ready to fire him on the spot. But when I looked into his eyes, I saw something familiar behind them: the reflection of another time and place.

Then Bob smiled at me and said, "Hello, Amy. It's me . . . *Clifford.*"

"More lies!" I shouted. "You *can't* be Clifford. He died in 1963 trying to save President Kennedy."

"I didn't die like the papers said. It's true, I did try to stop the assassination, and I did get shot. But I survived my injuries. Had I saved Kennedy, I would have been honored as a national hero, but my failure was sure to brand me as a national disgrace. The Media would have hounded me for the rest of my life. The doctors at the hospital were sympathetic, and forged a fake death certificate. I changed my name and went on to live a normal life."

Bob reached into his coat pocket and produced an admission pass to Theme Farm.

"But I also had the benefit of 20/20 hindsight," he continued. "I knew about Theme Farm and Used-to-Be TV. I waited by the attraction for days after it opened, knowing I'd see you at some point—and I did! Only then did I realize who you were. When I learned of your legal dispute with your parents, I knew I had to break my silence."

Judge Higgins held up Bob's documents. "It's all here, Amy, including depositions signed by each doctor who treated him in the '60s, and there is no question as to their authenticity. It's an incredible story, but Mr. Phillips' family relationship to you is irrefutable. And given the circumstances, I have decided to reverse my own decision. I therefore award custody of Amy to—"

Just then the courtroom doors banged open!

"No you don't!"

It was my dad, in a wheelchair, being pushed by

my mom, followed by my brother and sister.

"No one's going to take our Amy away from us!" shouted Dad, wheeling himself up to the judge.

"Your honor, this thing should never have happened. There are disagreements in any family. Battles break out and can go on forever, unless somebody bends a little. We talked it over, and realized that we haven't been very fair to Amy. Although to be honest, she's been no saint, either. But oddly, throughout all this, there was a spark—a kind of family connection that can never be broken. I for one would like to see a little more of that spark. I want it to burst into flames and warm our hearts the way it used to."

I approached my dad and looked down on him in his wheelchair.

"Do I know you?" I said. "You look like the man I'm doing battle with in court, but you sound like a father I used to love and admire. What made you change your mind?"

"In the hospital. Call it a vision, or a near-death experience, but my mind was on another plain. I heard beautiful sounds, and saw colors so vivid I can't describe them. Then I saw the light everyone talks about just before you die. I was drawn to its brilliance, and started to walk into it. Then I heard a voice. It said, *'Go back!'* Someone was standing in the light, blocking my way. It was you, Amy. I reached out, but you pushed me away. *'You don't belong here!'* you said. Next thing, I was staring up at the ceiling in my hospital room."

Mom approached the bench. "I don't know how or why, your honor, but somewhere along the way we went from *'we can't stand having Amy around'* to *'we can't live without her.'*"

What a twist! There I was, not wanted by anyone, then suddenly wanted by *everyone!*

The judge scratched his head and looked at me.

"Well, Amy," he said, "it seems that this is far from being an open-and-shut case. We can continue with it if you want, but I will need time to reconsider all these new developments."

"That won't be necessary, Judge," said Bob. "I think Amy can settle this right now."

I looked around the courtroom; at my adoptive parents and half-siblings, the only family I'd ever known; at Bob, my flesh-and-blood grandfather. Then I looked at the judge, who hadn't once displayed an ounce of emotion, smiling at me.

"Your honor," I said, "this is all happening so fast, I can hardly make sense of it. Someone very dear to me once said that you can't choose where, when, or to whom you will enter this world. But I know that spark Dad is talking about. I felt it—strangely, while I was most angry with him. It was trying to get out, but I had buried it so deep inside me that I couldn't find it. I have an affection for Clifford that will stay with me always, but that bond I have with my family can't be ignored. The world is full of unwanted children. Mom and Dad wanted me, and were willing to make the sacrifices necessary to raise me. How can I dismiss that?"

I embraced my mom. "I'm sorry for everything," I said.

"No sorrier than I am," she replied. Then she slipped something into my hand: Dad's bubble gum dispenser ring. "I'd like to finish that conversation we started."

"Hot chocolate tonight?" I said.

"It's a date!"

I hugged my dad, too.

"Guess what?" he said. "I'm starting a new novel. I'm calling it *Amy vs. The Dworlocks*."

"Really?" I said. "Who wins?"

"Don't know yet. I'm leaning toward the Dworlocks."

"C'mon, Dad. Give Amy a break."

"Well, okay. I'll give her superpowers."

I flung my arms around my sister.

"Eeeew!" she said, creeped out by my sudden intimacy.

"It gets worse," I said. Then I kissed her on the cheek.

My brother was next. I was surprised to feel his arms clutching my shoulders.

"Ya know," he said, "if you ever want to play video games with me . . ."

"Eeeew!" I said, revolted. "Tell you what. I'll give it a try, but you'll have to come out with me sometimes. You know? Outdoors? Sunlight?"

Judge Higgins stood up. "Alright, Amy, we're all warm and fuzzy now, but the court's time is valuable. I need your decision."

"Isn't there something in the law called visitation rights?" I asked him.

"With child custody battles in a divorce, yes. What are you proposing?"

"I get to stay with Bob . . . Clifford . . . or whatever his name is, from time to time, if it's okay with my parents, of course."

Dad wheeled himself over to Clifford, shook his hand, and smiled.

"I think we can probably arrange that," said Dad.

It was then time to give Clifford his hug—the biggest one of all.

"I gotta admit," I said, "You're a damn good attorney after all, but I have a bone to pick with one of your clients."

"Who's that?" asked Bob.

"Your zebra magician friend. He was wrong. You *can* touch the past."

Chapter 19

Channel '89

The sender's name on the special delivery envelope read *Shankstonville Family Court*. I was late coming home from school, and no one had yet checked the mailbox. I opened the envelope and found a cover letter that began *RE: Joint Custody of a Minor Child*. More papers inside confirmed what Clifford and my folks had already agreed to. I would live with my adoptive parents, and stay with Clifford on prearranged dates throughout the year. Judge Higgins had thrown out my emancipation case, and accepted my joint custody petition. Clifford had filed all the paperwork—pro bono, of course.

My family and I had prepared a separate agreement of our own. Though not legally binding in the eyes of the court, we would adopt a spirit of compromise. The family would be more considerate of my wishes, and I promised to do the same for them. A system was worked out that everyone could live with. Restrictions were imposed on how much TV my parents could watch—ironically, a rule usually reserved for teenagers. How many hours my brother and sister could spend in cyber activities was also limited. Family vacations were worked into the schedule as well. There was a bit of moaning at first, but once the system was tested, no one had any objections.

I opened our front door while examining the documents, but as I passed over the threshold, I thought I had gone into the wrong house. It was dead quiet, as if my family had vacated the premises. There were no sound effects blasting from the living room TV; no alien explosions from my brother's video games; no loud gabbing on the phone from my sister. I glanced at the address on the door to be sure I hadn't accidentally wandered into a neighbor's house.

I crept toward the living room, then came upon a startling sight: my dad sitting quietly, reading a book! He looked perfectly relaxed in his recliner chair, under a reading lamp that hadn't once been turned on. His doctor was trying to keep Dad's stress levels in check, and it was decided that reading was the best medicine for him.

Dad's health had improved significantly since his heart attack. He was even permitted to go on morning runs, so long as he promised to wear a heart rate monitor. I kept Dad honest by accompanying him on his Sunday outings.

"Got the mail, Dad," I said.

"I'll be with you in a minute," he said, his eyes locked on his book. "Gotta finish this chapter."

"What are you reading?"

He held up the cover without lifting his eyes off the page. He was reading *To Kill a Mockingbird*.

The stillness in the upstairs hallway was creepy. Not a grumble nor a groan came through the doors of my sibling's bedrooms. Then I heard the sound of a motor out the window to the backyard. I looked outside and almost fainted. My brother was mowing the lawn, and my sister was pruning the rose bushes. Maybe I *was* in the wrong house after all!

I entered my attic bedroom to find the family photo album laying on my bed. A note was taped to the cover that read *Welcome back! Love you, Mom*. Thumbing through the album revealed that all my old photos were back where they belonged. My birth certificate was there, too—the unaltered one, showing my real birth mother's name, Mary.

Something smelled great downstairs.

I went to the kitchen, and was shocked to find pots and pans on the stove. Sauces, fresh vegetables, and a beef stew simmered on its glowing burners. The light in the oven was on. I looked through its window. Oatmeal cookies!

Then my dad walked in and saw me. He jumped

as if I had caught him committing a crime or something.

"Just checking on dinner," he said, like he did this kind of thing all the time.

"And since when do you cook?" I asked.

"Some of the best chefs in the world are men. Did you know that? The days of chaining your wife to the stove went out with the '60s. Besides, I *like* cooking."

Then mom entered, humming as she sauntered over to the stove. She sampled the savory stew with a wooden spoon. "Mmm," she said, smacking her lips.

Then Mom turned to me. "Go wash up for dinner, dear," she said.

"Wash up?" I said with a smirk. "What is this, the Cleaver household?"

Mom smirked back at me and pointed the way to the bathroom.

I had created a monster! My rants about the joys of living like a mid-century family had exploded in my face. All I was asking for was a little normalcy. What I got was *Opie!*

The kitchen was empty when I returned.

"In here, honey," I heard my mom say. I walked into the dining room, an area that had never been used for which it was designed. There was my whole family, sitting up straight with napkins in their laps, around a beautiful table with the price tag still hanging from it. Long candles flickered above a flowery centerpiece.

They all smiled at me as I came through the door. It was like I had entered the *Twilight Zone* —trapped in a '60s family TV show.

"Aren't you forgetting someone?" I said. "Where's *Beaver?* Washing up?"

"Beaver's out on his paper route," said my dad. "That leaves an empty chair. Care to join us?"

It was the perfect ending to an amazing adventure. I had altered history, traveled to legal hell and back, and discovered my true heritage—all to serve one wish: to get as far away from my family as I could. Now, there they were, as lovable as a Norman Rockwell painting, and I couldn't think of anywhere else I would rather be.

I sat down between my brother and sister, with Mom and Dad beaming at me across a scrumptious, home-cooked meal. I didn't know how long this Wally-and-Beaver world would last. Sooner or later, the 21st century would catch up with us, and the group dinners and paper routes would all come to an end. But for now, I was an *orphan in wonderland*. And as I dug my fork into my mash potatoes, I realized who I was truly dining with that evening:

The family I always wanted.

"Pass the gravy, please."

The screams of a hundred teenage girls nearly

knocked us over, as Hubert, Clifford, and I entered Theme Farm. An outdoor stage was set up just inside the main gate. Performing onstage was a Fritter version of a pop music boy band: *3PiG*. They were playing their latest hit, and the newest song written by Clifford:

"Bring Us Home, Sweet Mary"

> *So get on board and we're on our way*
> *Time gets nearer the more we delay*
> *Sweet Mary please, bring us home*

> *It's a long way to Dorian*
> *Such a long way to go, so*
> *Sweet Mary please, bring us home*

An alarm sounded from Hubert's tablet, alerting him that a Theme Farm show was about to begin.

"Fireworks in ten minutes," he said. "Anyone coming with me?"

"You go ahead," I said. "How about we meet up at the *Illegal Alien* for lunch afterward?"

"Sí, sí, Señorita Amy."

Then off he went.

Clifford and I casually explored the park on our own with no set agenda.

I unfolded a Theme Farm guide map. "Here's a ride an attorney would like," I said. I read Clifford the description. *"Puppets Court: Frog puppet prosecutes corrupt U.S. congressman accused of accepting kick-backs."*

"I've seen it," said Clifford. "The congressman walks free, and gets reelected for a fourth term. That's puppet justice for you."

Then we passed an attraction we both knew all too well: Used-to-Be TV. A banner hung above the newly refurbished entrance that read: *Channel '89 Now Open!*

I pretended not to notice it, staring down at my guide map. I was in no hurry to relive that experience, given the emotional toll it took on me the last time.

But Clifford had other plans.

"Let's go in," he said.

"Do I have to?" I asked. "I feel kinda creepy about that place."

"For old times' sake."

"Oh . . . alright."

The '60s, ranch-style house had been transformed into a household of the 1980s. The interior now matched the year that guests would be looking in on: *1989*. Each room of the house offered a glimpse at '80s pop culture. Cabbage Patch Kids lay on the beds in the children's room, with an unsolved Rubik's Cube on the dresser. Vinyl record albums by The Bangles, Blondie, and George Michael leaned up against a huge ghetto blaster in the teen's room. The family room featured the ultimate in '80s entertainment: a full-sized Pac-Man arcade console.

As before, the automatic garage door opened onto the neighborhood street with the perpetual sunset. We strolled down the block, checking out the updated cottages.

"There's an empty one," said Clifford, pointing to the very cottage he and I used when he was a '60s teenager.

We went inside and sat down on a green, velveteen couch. The TV came on—now in "living color." On the screen was the inside of a huge TV studio in 1989. Muslin backdrops leaned against the walls. Various props were stacked on shelves. The only person in the room was a cleaning woman mopping the floor at the back of the studio.

"Call that girl over," said Clifford.

"You think I should?" I said.

"Sure. Why not?"

"Excuse me, ma'am?" I called out toward the screen.

"You called me?" said the woman, her distant voice echoing through the open space.

"Come here, would you please?"

The woman jammed her mop into a bucket, and walked toward us. She was younger than I thought —about my age, actually, and pretty as a peach.

"Oh, hello, Mr. Smith," she said to Clifford.

"Back again?"

"Mr. Smith?" I said to Clifford with suspicion in my voice. "What are you up to?"

Clifford held up his hand to hush me up, then said to the girl on the screen: "I have someone here who wants to meet you."

"What are you talking about?" I asked Clifford. "I didn't ask to meet—"

"Sure you did," he said, winking at me. Then he pointed to the screen and grinned. "I'd like you to meet . . . *Mary.*"

I had heard that name spoken in court. Clifford had named his daughter Mary—who turned out to be my . . .

"Mary?" I said staring at Clifford with my mouth hanging open.

"Yes," he replied, his smile broader now.

"Mary?" I said again.

Clifford grabbed my head and rotated it to face the TV screen.

Her hair. Her eyes. All of her facial features were just like my own.

Ohmigod!

She was my *mother!*

"Say something to Mary," said Clifford.

Mary tilted her head and scratched her nose, patiently waiting for me to speak.

But what could I say? There was my real mother in 1989, the same age as me. For sure, she didn't know me from Adam. Knowing that my birth would mean the end of her life was profoundly disturbing. I couldn't decide if meeting her was a gift or a curse.

"It's okay," said Clifford. "Trust me."

My heart raced as I started to speak. "N-nice to meet you, Mary," I said. "I'm *(bleep)*."

"I beg your pardon," said Mary. "I didn't catch that."

I tugged at Clifford's sleeve with tears in my eyes. "Why are you doing this?" I said. "Can't you see this is killing me?"

Then Clifford pulled a small object from his pocket. In his hand was the magic clicker, all scratched and dented.

"Hubert fished it out of the lake the day after you threw it in there," he said. "He took the thing apart and was somehow able to fix it. Genius, that kid."

Then Clifford stood up and handed me the device.

"I think I'll leave you two alone," he said. "But remember: one wrong word and you might suddenly disappear."

I held the clicker up over my head, like I had found the Holy Grail, just as the door closed behind me.

"What were you two saying?" asked Mary.

"Nothing important," I said.

I took a long look at Mary, as my smile chased away the last tear.

"Hello Mary," I said, then aimed the clicker at the screen.

Click!

"My name's Amy."

About the Author

Bruce Edwards was born in Marin County, California and raised on a tasty diet of jazz and Disney animation. He majored in Architecture in college, but switched to Music to join the burgeoning San Francisco music scene. As a composer and musician, he wrote rock tunes and radio jingles, and toured as a pop music artist between studio gigs. He tinkered with early computer animation which led to a career as a feature film character animator. His more unique vocational detours included a stint as a puppeteer and performing magic at Disneyland. As a writer, he wrote screenplays during his Hollywood years before finding an audience for his young-adult fiction. Mr. Edwards currently lives in Orange County, California.

YOU KNOW THE SONGS
NOW HEAR THE MUSIC!

"Your Love, Like Music" and the other songs in this book were actually written some 40 years ago, and were the key inspiration for *The Age of Amy: Channel '63*.

Hear the re-recordings of theses vintage tunes, composed and performed by author Bruce Edwards.

AUDIO CLIPS
MUSIC VIDEOS
DOWNLOADS
AND MORE!

www.AgeOfAmy.com/songs

AMY GOES TO WASHINGTON!

The Age of Amy:
The Thumper Amendment

BOOK #2 IN THE SERIES

"Welcome to
the world
of meanness."

Amy joins a presidential campaign in this fantasy-adventure through the bizarre world of American politics.

"Readers will appreciate Amy's sharp wit
and the overall comedy of political theater"
— *Booklist*

Lambert Hill

WHERE IT ALL BEGINS!

The Age of Amy:
Bonehead Bootcamp

BOOK #1 IN THE SERIES

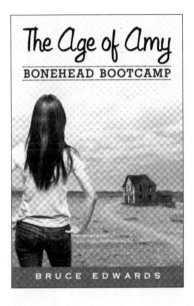

"To be perfectly
honest, I don't think
I belong here."

Amy is unjustly sent to a boot camp for troubled teens where she discovers a frightening fantasy world.

> *"The Age of Amy: Bonehead Bootcamp* is truly a book about finding one's real self. I highly recommend this book."
> — *All Books Review*